Sir Arthur Conan Doyle's

The **Adventure** of the **Second Stain**

Adapted by: Vincent Goodwin

Illustrated by: Ben Dunn

magic
wagon

visit us at
www.abdopublishing.com

Published by Magic Wagon, a division of the ABDO Group, PO Box 398166, Minneapolis, Minnesota, 55439. Copyright © 2014 by Abdo Consulting Group, Inc. International copyrights reserved in all countries. All rights reserved. No part of this book may be reproduced in any form without written permission from the publisher.

Graphic Planet™ is a trademark and logo of Magic Wagon.

Printed in the United States of America, North Mankato, Minnesota.
052013
092013
 This book contains at least 10% recycled materials.

Written by Sir Arthur Conan Doyle
Adapted by Vincent Goodwin
Illustrated by Ben Dunn
Colored by Robby Bevard
Lettered by Doug Dlin
Edited by Stephanie Hedlund and Rochelle Baltzer
Interior layout by Antarctic Press
Cover art by Ben Dunn
Cover design by Abbey Fitzgerald

Library of Congress Cataloging-in-Publication Data

Goodwin, Vincent.
  Sir Arthur Conan Doyle's The adventure of the second stain / adapted by Vincent Goodwin ; illustrated by Ben Dunn.
      p. cm. -- (The graphic novel adventures of Sherlock Holmes)
  Summary: Retold in graphic novel form, Sherlock Holmes is called in by the Prime Minister to solve the mystery when an important document disappears from a locked box in the home of the Secretary for European Affairs.
  ISBN 978-1-61641-975-2
1. Doyle, Arthur Conan, Sir, 1859-1930. Adventure of the second stain--Adaptations. 2. Holmes, Sherlock (Fictitious character)--Comic books, strips, etc. 3. Holmes, Sherlock (Fictitious character)--Juvenile fiction. 4. Graphic novels. [1. Graphic novels. 2. Doyle, Arthur Conan, Sir, 1859-1930. Adventure of the second stain--Adaptations. 3. Mystery and detective stories.] I. Dunn, Ben, ill. II. Doyle, Arthur Conan, Sir, 1859-1930. Adventure of the second stain. III. Title. IV. Title: Adventure of the second stain.
  PZ7.7.G66Sirf 2013
   741.5'973--dc23
                                                              2013004376

Table of Contents

Cast

Sherlock Holmes

Dr. John Watson

Trelawney Hope

Hilda Hope

Inspector Lestrade

Lord Bellinger

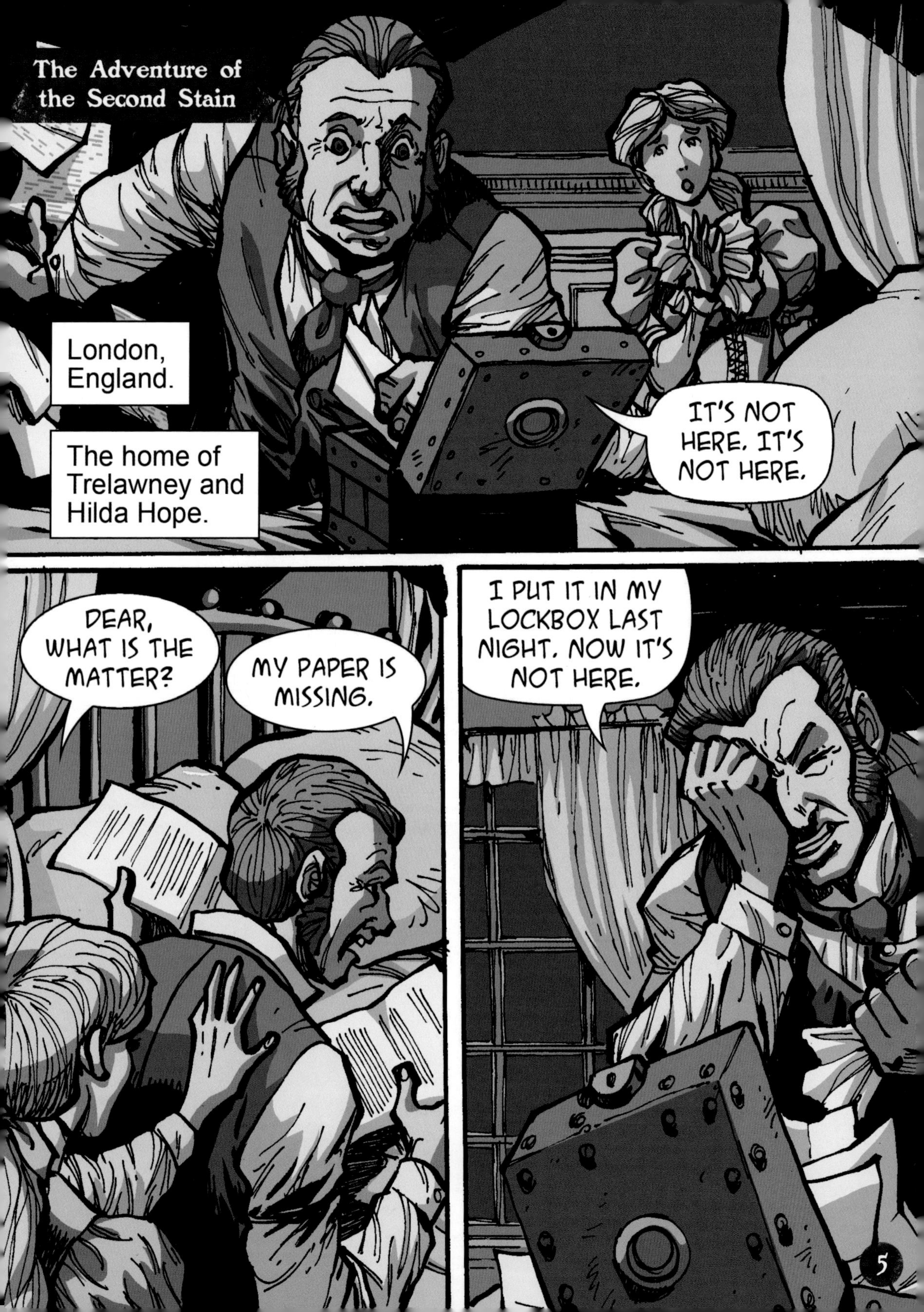
The Adventure of the Second Stain
London, England.
The home of Trelawney and Hilda Hope.
IT'S NOT HERE. IT'S NOT HERE.
DEAR, WHAT IS THE MATTER?
MY PAPER IS MISSING.
I PUT IT IN MY LOCKBOX LAST NIGHT. NOW IT'S NOT HERE.

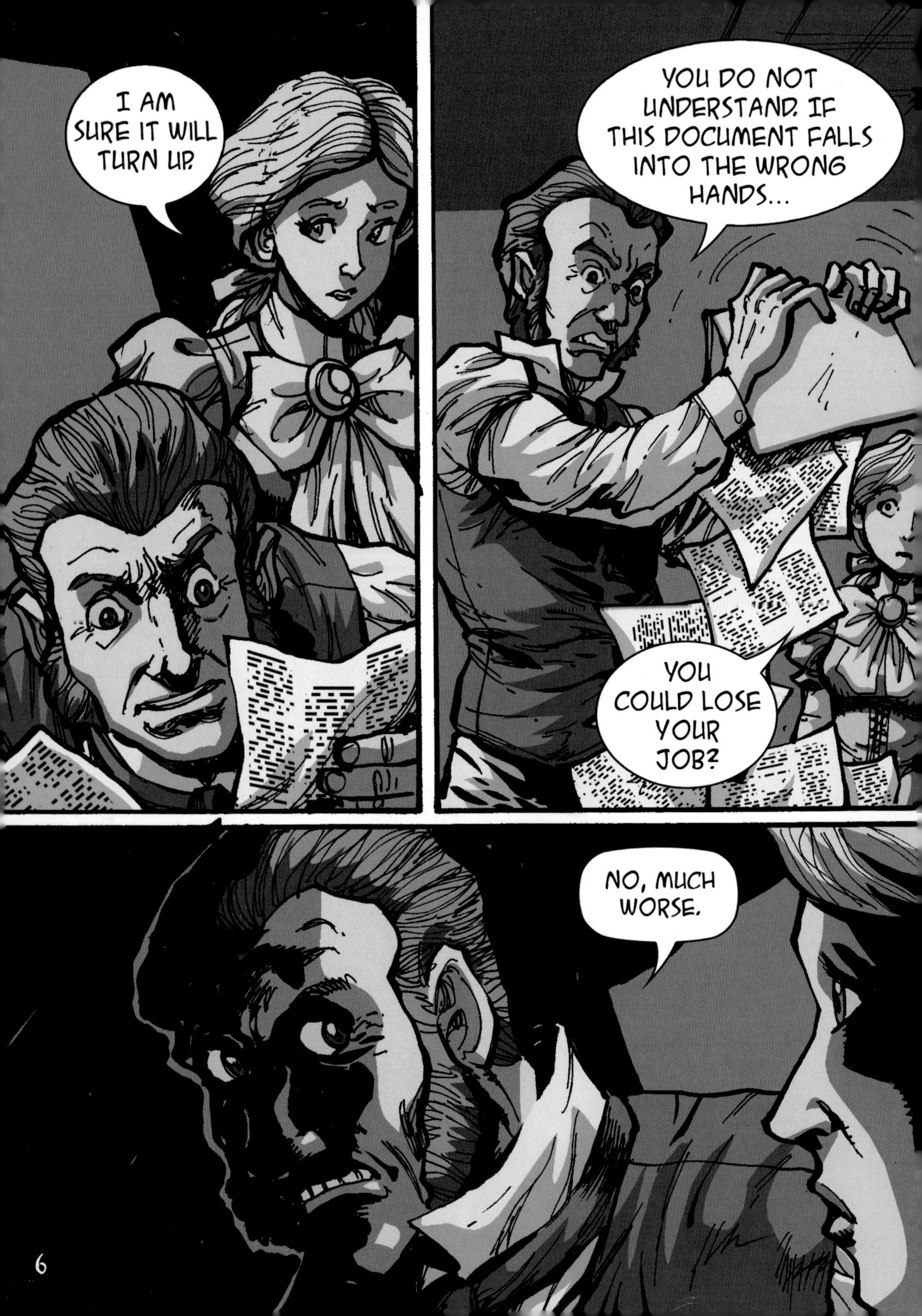
I AM SURE IT WILL TURN UP.
YOU DO NOT UNDERSTAND. IF THIS DOCUMENT FALLS INTO THE WRONG HANDS...
YOU COULD LOSE YOUR JOB?
NO, MUCH WORSE.

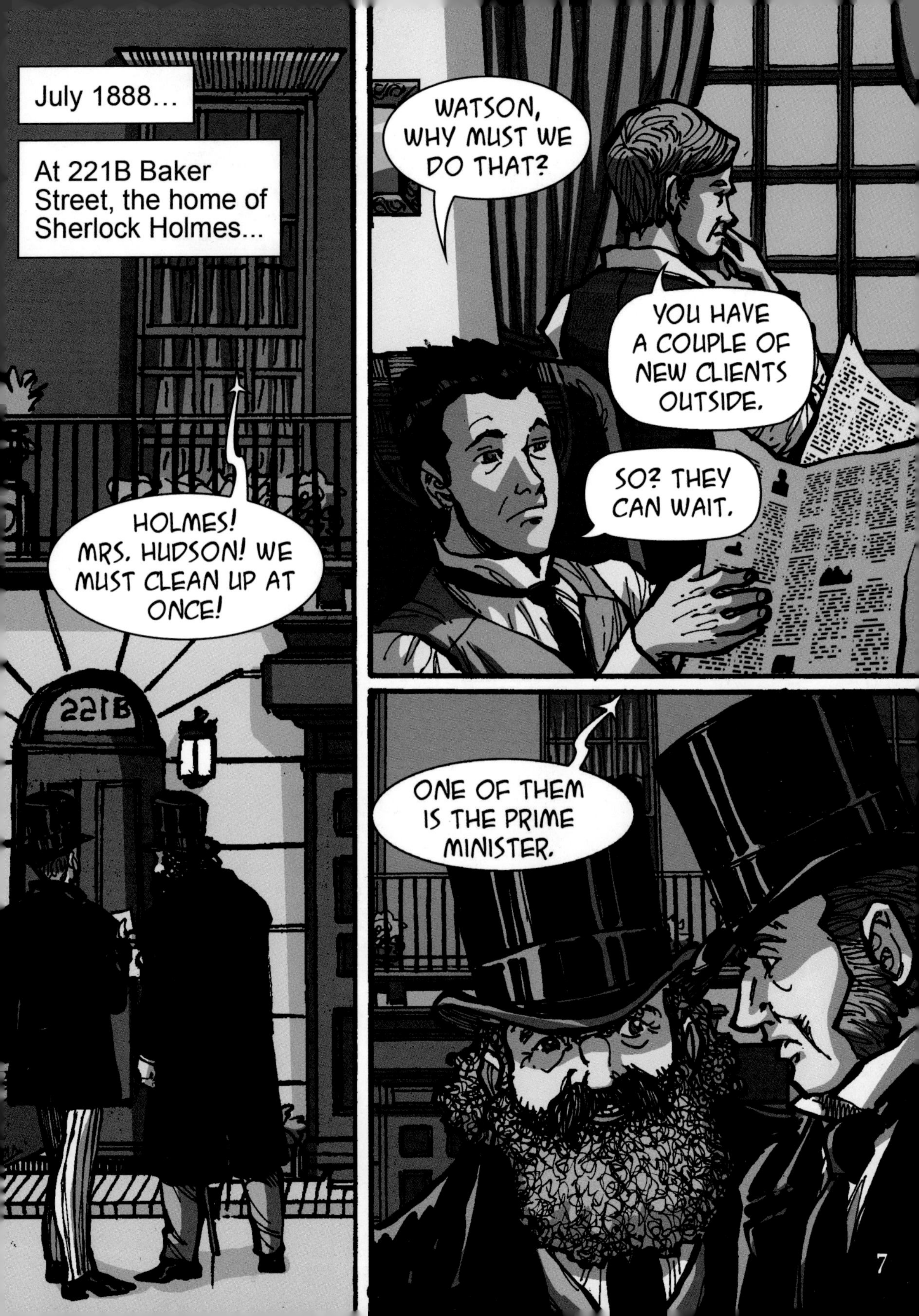
July 1888…
At 221B Baker Street, the home of Sherlock Holmes...
221B
HOLMES! MRS. HUDSON! WE MUST CLEAN UP AT ONCE!
WATSON, WHY MUST WE DO THAT?
YOU HAVE A COUPLE OF NEW CLIENTS OUTSIDE.
SO? THEY CAN WAIT.
ONE OF THEM IS THE PRIME MINISTER.

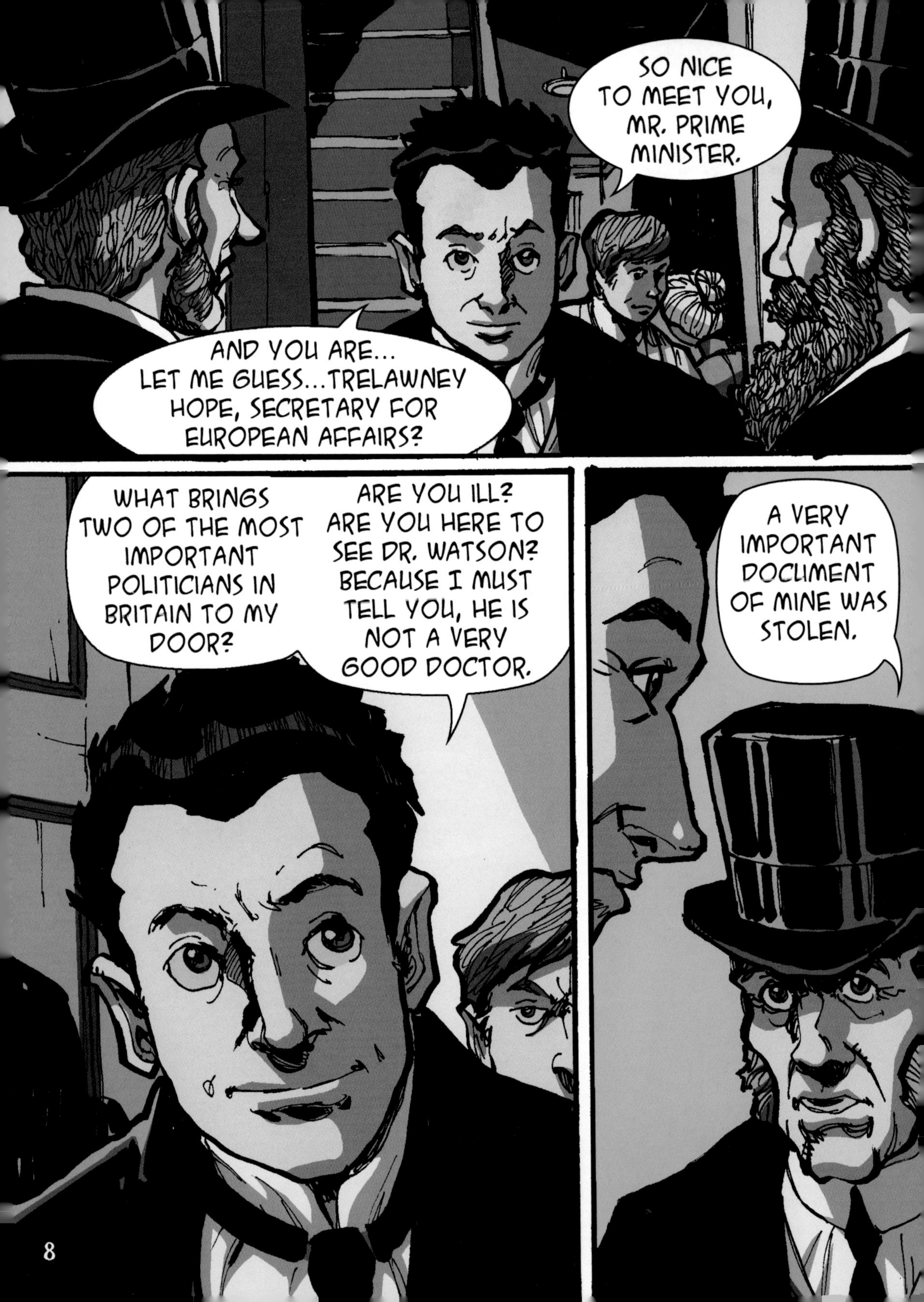
SO NICE TO MEET YOU, MR. PRIME MINISTER.
AND YOU ARE... LET ME GUESS...TRELAWNEY HOPE, SECRETARY FOR EUROPEAN AFFAIRS?
WHAT BRINGS TWO OF THE MOST IMPORTANT POLITICIANS IN BRITAIN TO MY DOOR?
ARE YOU ILL? ARE YOU HERE TO SEE DR. WATSON? BECAUSE I MUST TELL YOU, HE IS NOT A VERY GOOD DOCTOR.
A VERY IMPORTANT DOCUMENT OF MINE WAS STOLEN.

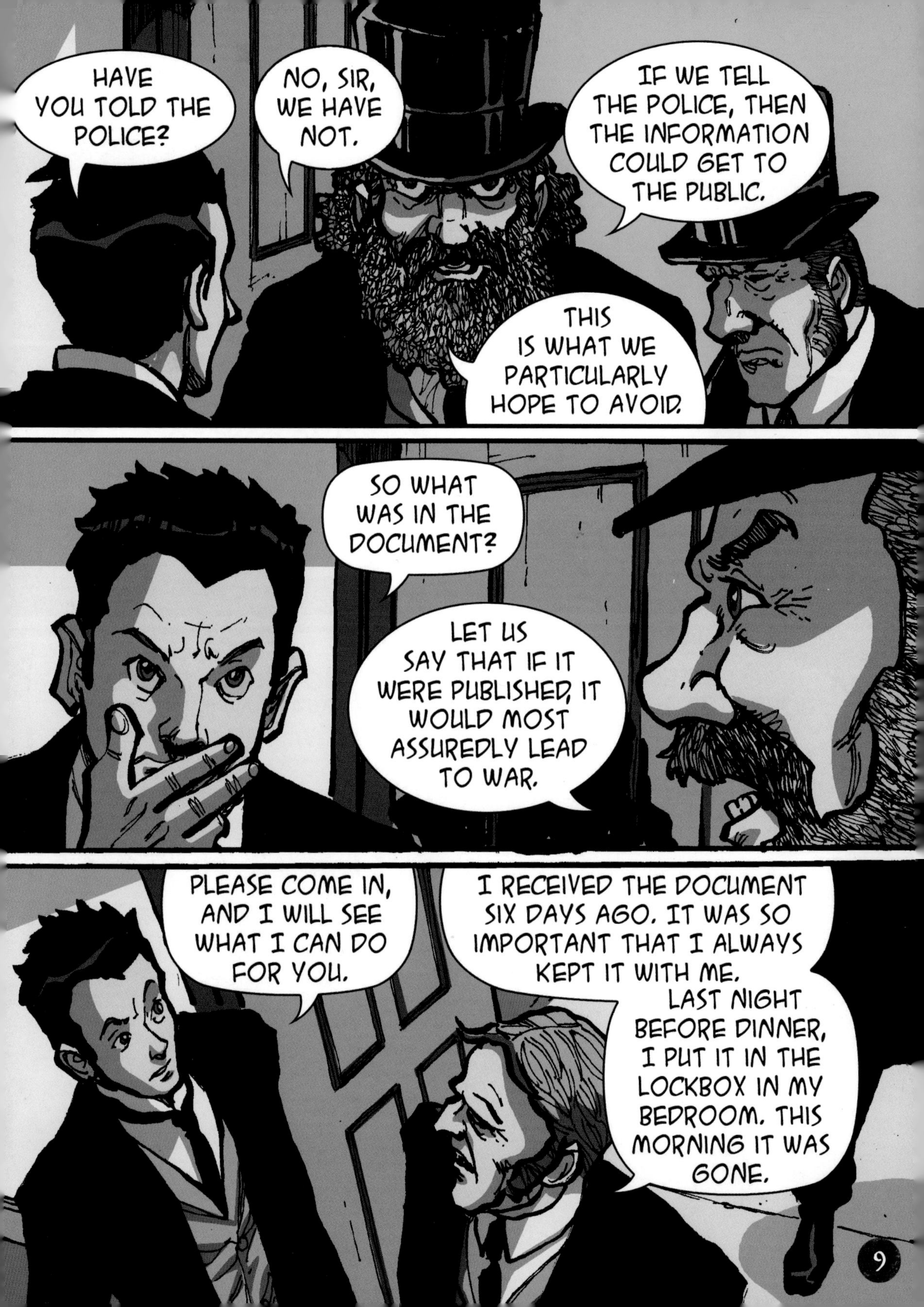

HAVE YOU TOLD THE POLICE?
NO, SIR, WE HAVE NOT.
IF WE TELL THE POLICE, THEN THE INFORMATION COULD GET TO THE PUBLIC.
THIS IS WHAT WE PARTICULARLY HOPE TO AVOID.
SO WHAT WAS IN THE DOCUMENT?
LET US SAY THAT IF IT WERE PUBLISHED, IT WOULD MOST ASSUREDLY LEAD TO WAR.
PLEASE COME IN, AND I WILL SEE WHAT I CAN DO FOR YOU.
I RECEIVED THE DOCUMENT SIX DAYS AGO. IT WAS SO IMPORTANT THAT I ALWAYS KEPT IT WITH ME.
LAST NIGHT BEFORE DINNER, I PUT IT IN THE LOCKBOX IN MY BEDROOM. THIS MORNING IT WAS GONE.

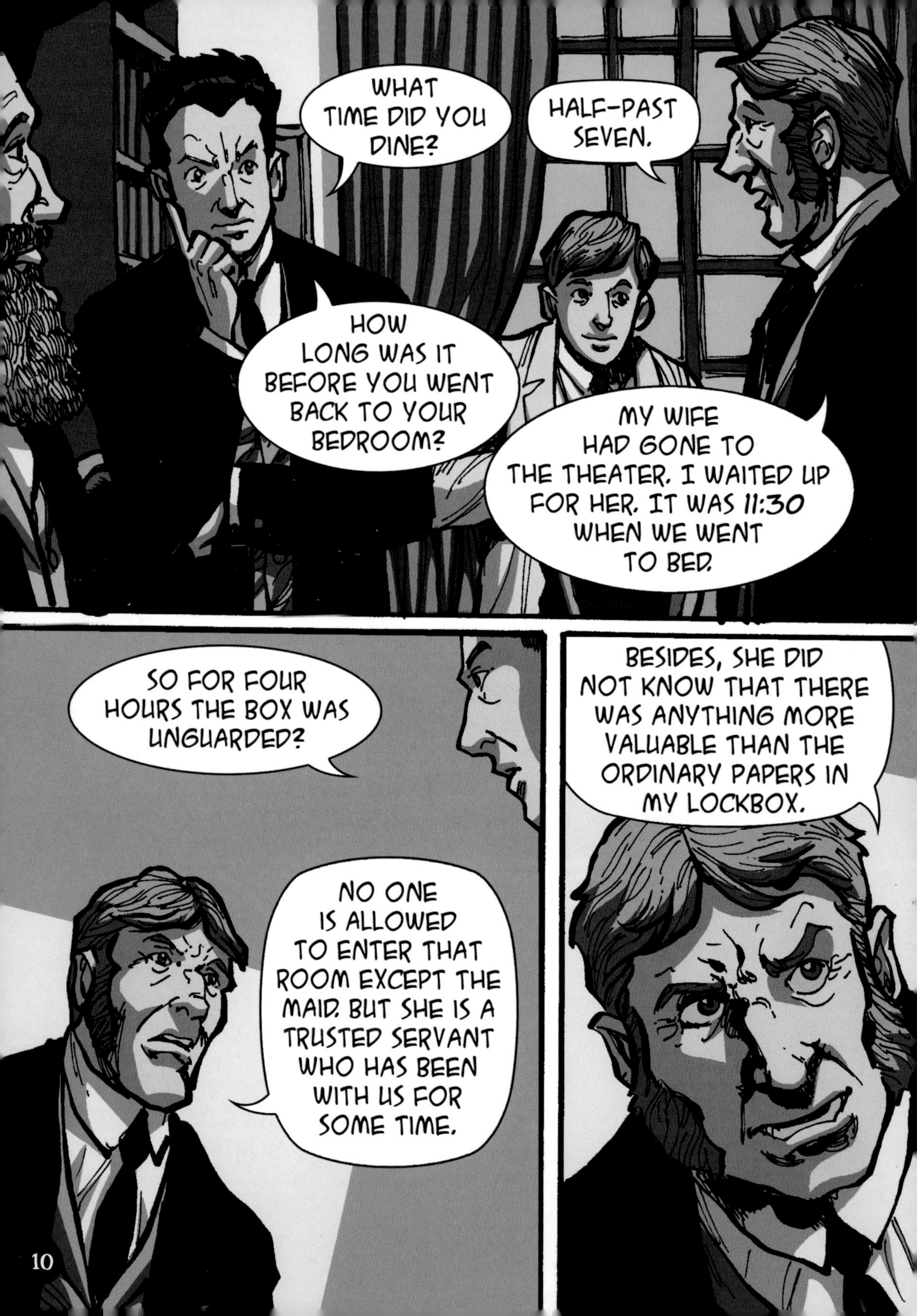
WHAT TIME DID YOU DINE?
HALF-PAST SEVEN.
HOW LONG WAS IT BEFORE YOU WENT BACK TO YOUR BEDROOM?
MY WIFE HAD GONE TO THE THEATER. I WAITED UP FOR HER. IT WAS 11:30 WHEN WE WENT TO BED.
SO FOR FOUR HOURS THE BOX WAS UNGUARDED?
NO ONE IS ALLOWED TO ENTER THAT ROOM EXCEPT THE MAID. BUT SHE IS A TRUSTED SERVANT WHO HAS BEEN WITH US FOR SOME TIME.
BESIDES, SHE DID NOT KNOW THAT THERE WAS ANYTHING MORE VALUABLE THAN THE ORDINARY PAPERS IN MY LOCKBOX.

MR. HOPE, COULD SOMEONE HAVE STOLEN IT WHILE YOU WERE ASLEEP?
I AM A LIGHT SLEEPER, AND SO IS MY WIFE. NO ONE COULD HAVE ENTERED THE ROOM DURING THE NIGHT.
7:30 PM
MORNING 11:30AM
11:30 PM
MORNING
SLEEPING
BUT THE PAPER IS GONE.
DID YOUR WIFE KNOW ABOUT THE DOCUMENT?
NO, SIR. I SAID NOTHING ABOUT IT TO MY WIFE UNTIL I SAW IT WAS MISSING THIS MORNING.
WHO ELSE KNOWS ABOUT THE LETTER?
NO ONE ELSE IN ENGLAND, I ASSURE YOU.

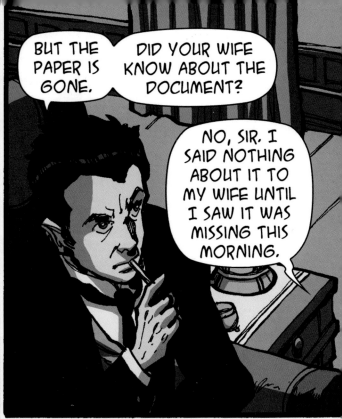

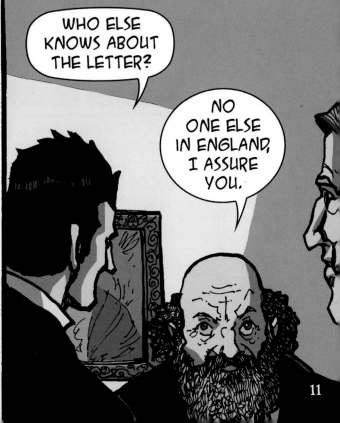

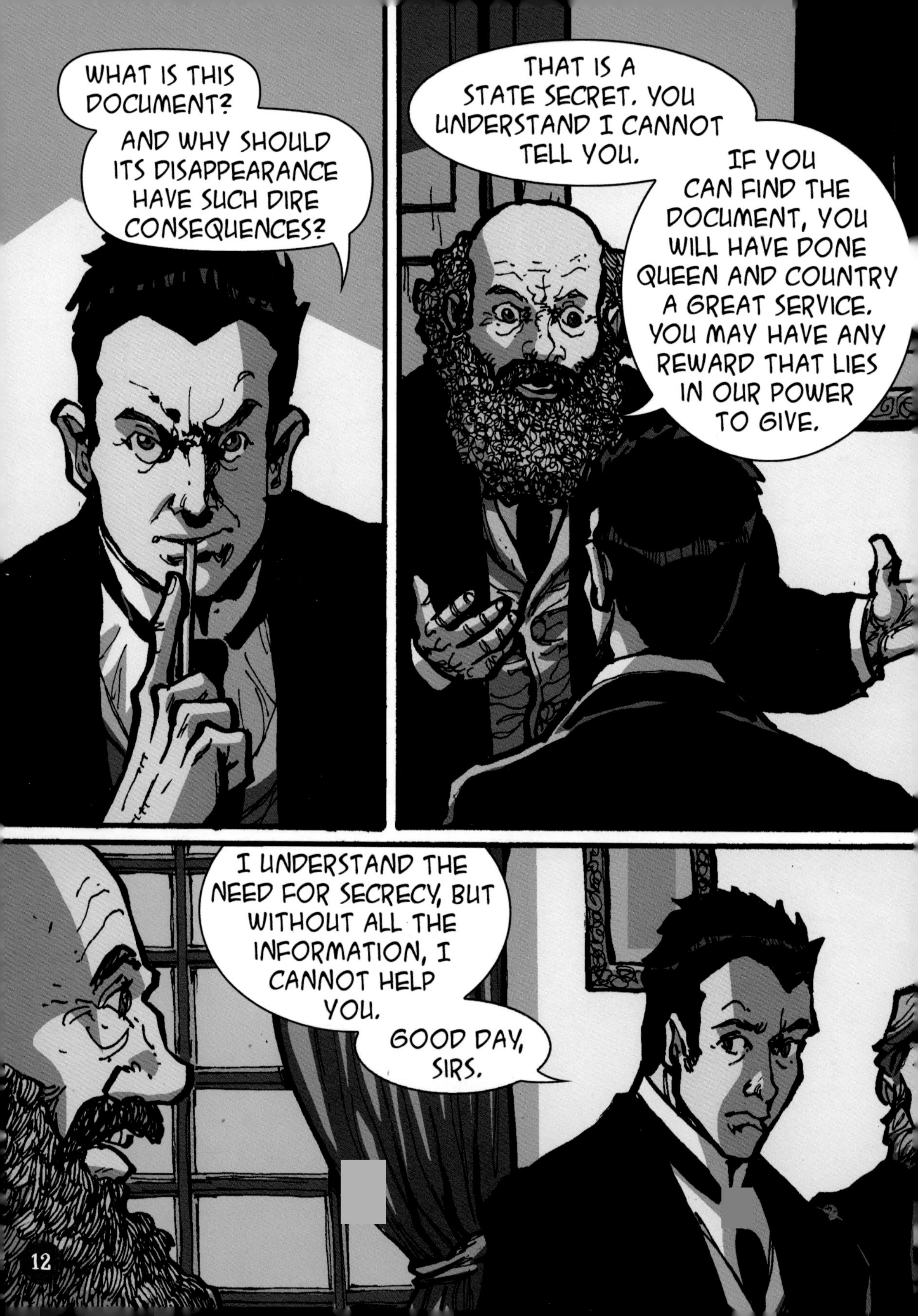
WHAT IS THIS DOCUMENT?
AND WHY SHOULD ITS DISAPPEARANCE HAVE SUCH DIRE CONSEQUENCES?
THAT IS A STATE SECRET. YOU UNDERSTAND I CANNOT TELL YOU.
IF YOU CAN FIND THE DOCUMENT, YOU WILL HAVE DONE QUEEN AND COUNTRY A GREAT SERVICE. YOU MAY HAVE ANY REWARD THAT LIES IN OUR POWER TO GIVE.
I UNDERSTAND THE NEED FOR SECRECY, BUT WITHOUT ALL THE INFORMATION, I CANNOT HELP YOU.
GOOD DAY, SIRS.

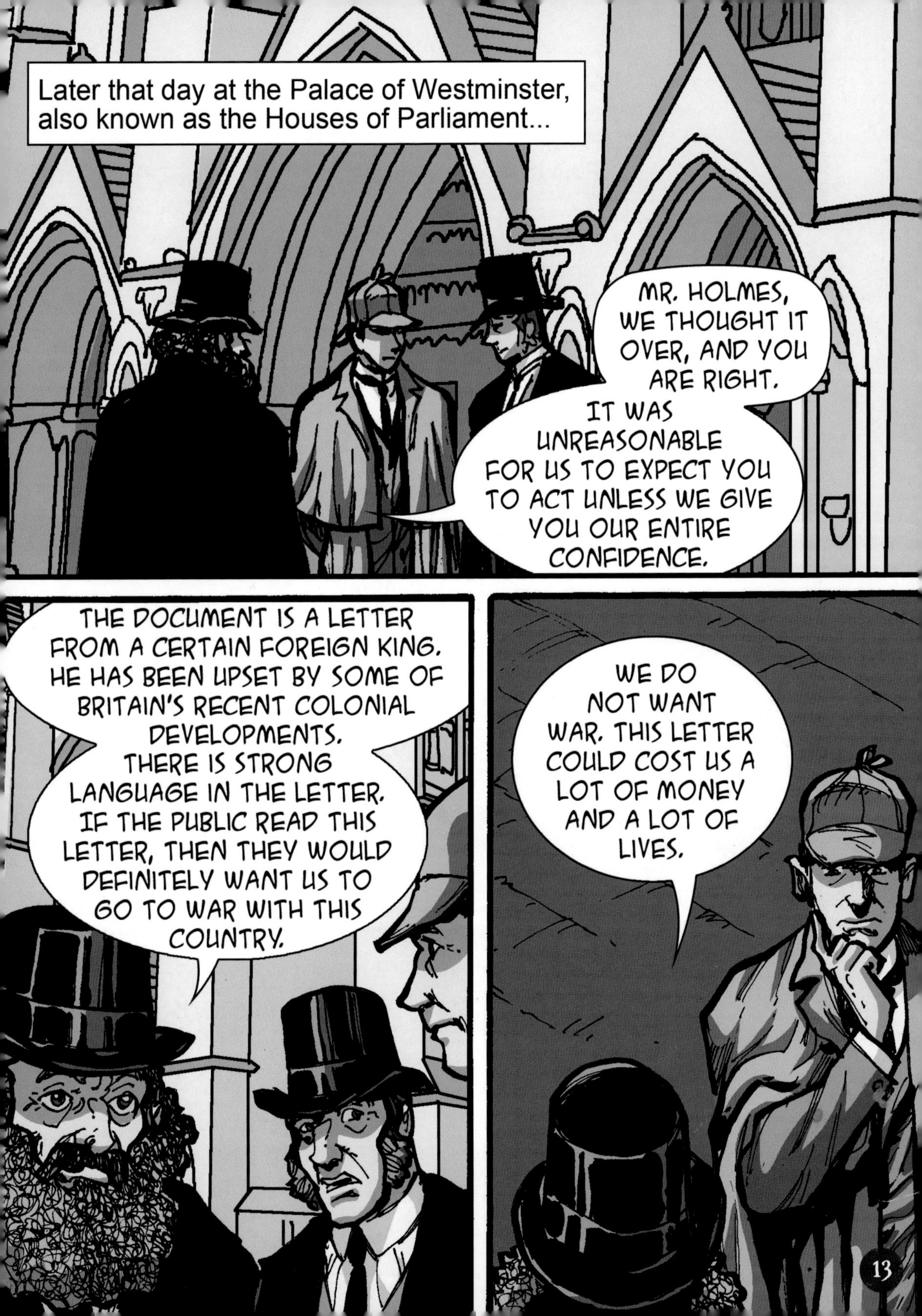

Later that day at the Palace of Westminster, also known as the Houses of Parliament...
MR. HOLMES, WE THOUGHT IT OVER, AND YOU ARE RIGHT.
IT WAS UNREASONABLE FOR US TO EXPECT YOU TO ACT UNLESS WE GIVE YOU OUR ENTIRE CONFIDENCE.
THE DOCUMENT IS A LETTER FROM A CERTAIN FOREIGN KING. HE HAS BEEN UPSET BY SOME OF BRITAIN'S RECENT COLONIAL DEVELOPMENTS.
THERE IS STRONG LANGUAGE IN THE LETTER. IF THE PUBLIC READ THIS LETTER, THEN THEY WOULD DEFINITELY WANT US TO GO TO WAR WITH THIS COUNTRY.
WE DO NOT WANT WAR. THIS LETTER COULD COST US A LOT OF MONEY AND A LOT OF LIVES.

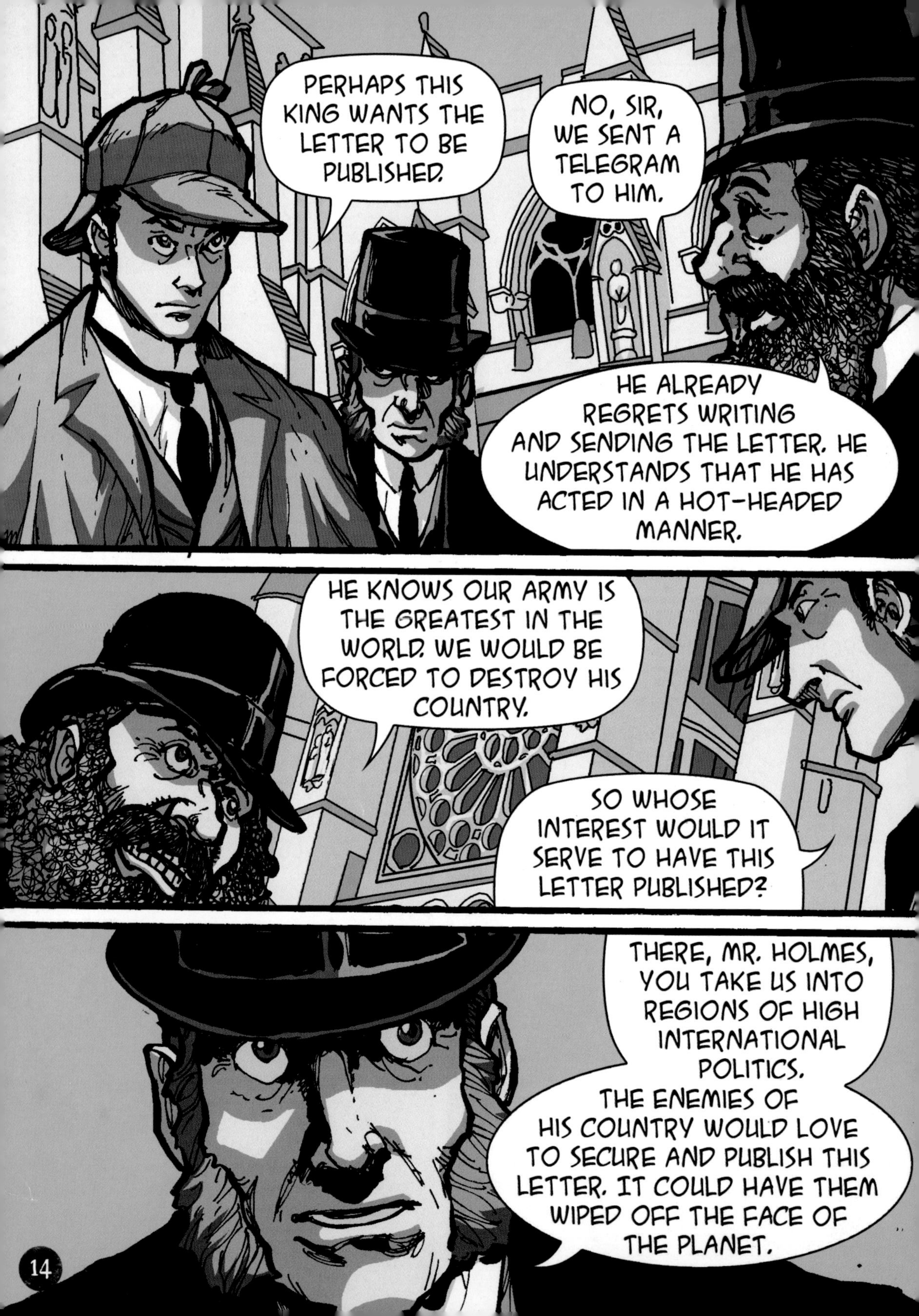
PERHAPS THIS KING WANTS THE LETTER TO BE PUBLISHED.
NO, SIR, WE SENT A TELEGRAM TO HIM.
HE ALREADY REGRETS WRITING AND SENDING THE LETTER. HE UNDERSTANDS THAT HE HAS ACTED IN A HOT-HEADED MANNER.
HE KNOWS OUR ARMY IS THE GREATEST IN THE WORLD. WE WOULD BE FORCED TO DESTROY HIS COUNTRY.
SO WHOSE INTEREST WOULD IT SERVE TO HAVE THIS LETTER PUBLISHED?
THERE, MR. HOLMES, YOU TAKE US INTO REGIONS OF HIGH INTERNATIONAL POLITICS.
THE ENEMIES OF HIS COUNTRY WOULD LOVE TO SECURE AND PUBLISH THIS LETTER. IT COULD HAVE THEM WIPED OFF THE FACE OF THE PLANET.

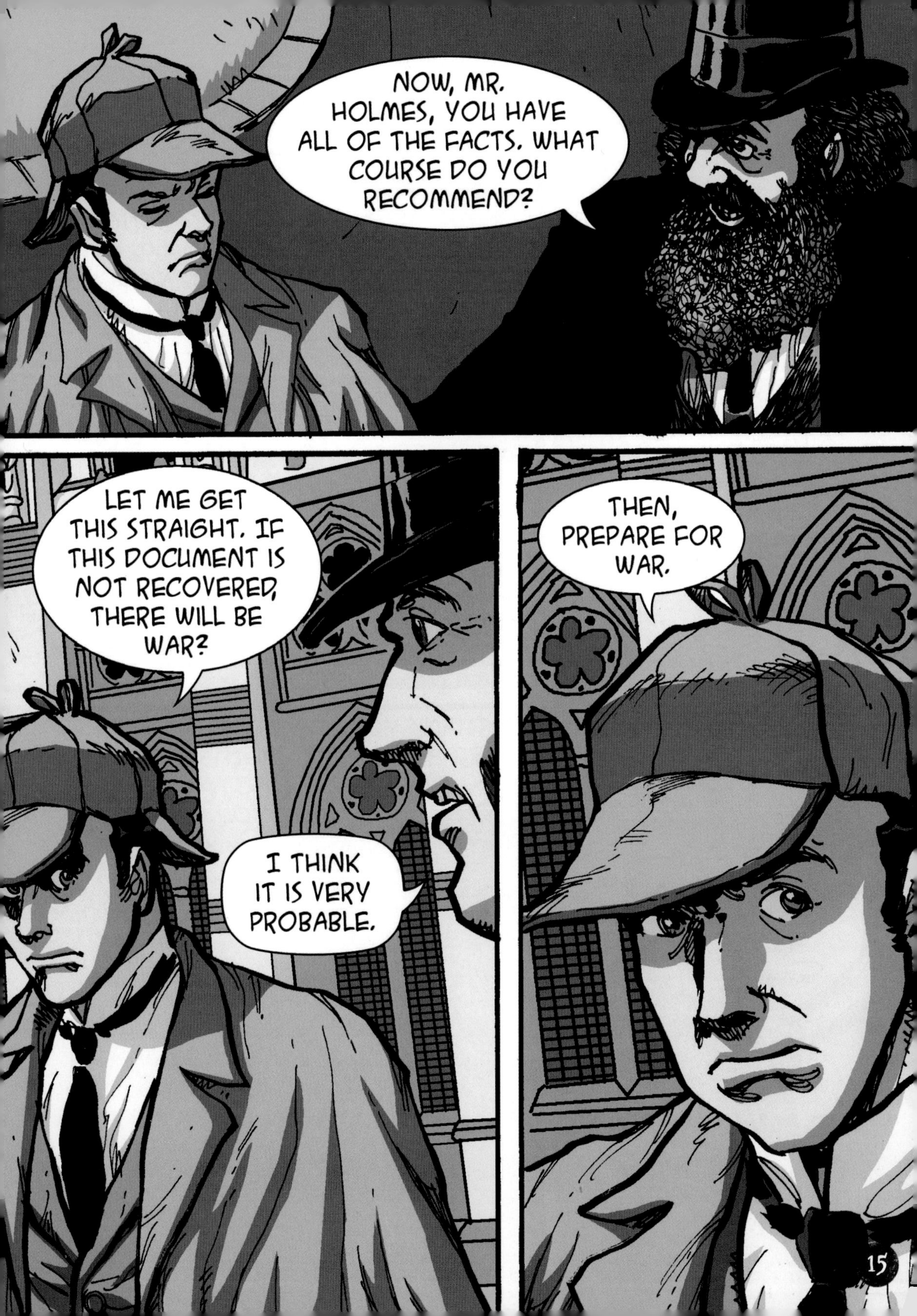
NOW, MR. HOLMES, YOU HAVE ALL OF THE FACTS. WHAT COURSE DO YOU RECOMMEND?
LET ME GET THIS STRAIGHT. IF THIS DOCUMENT IS NOT RECOVERED, THERE WILL BE WAR?
I THINK IT IS VERY PROBABLE.
THEN, PREPARE FOR WAR.

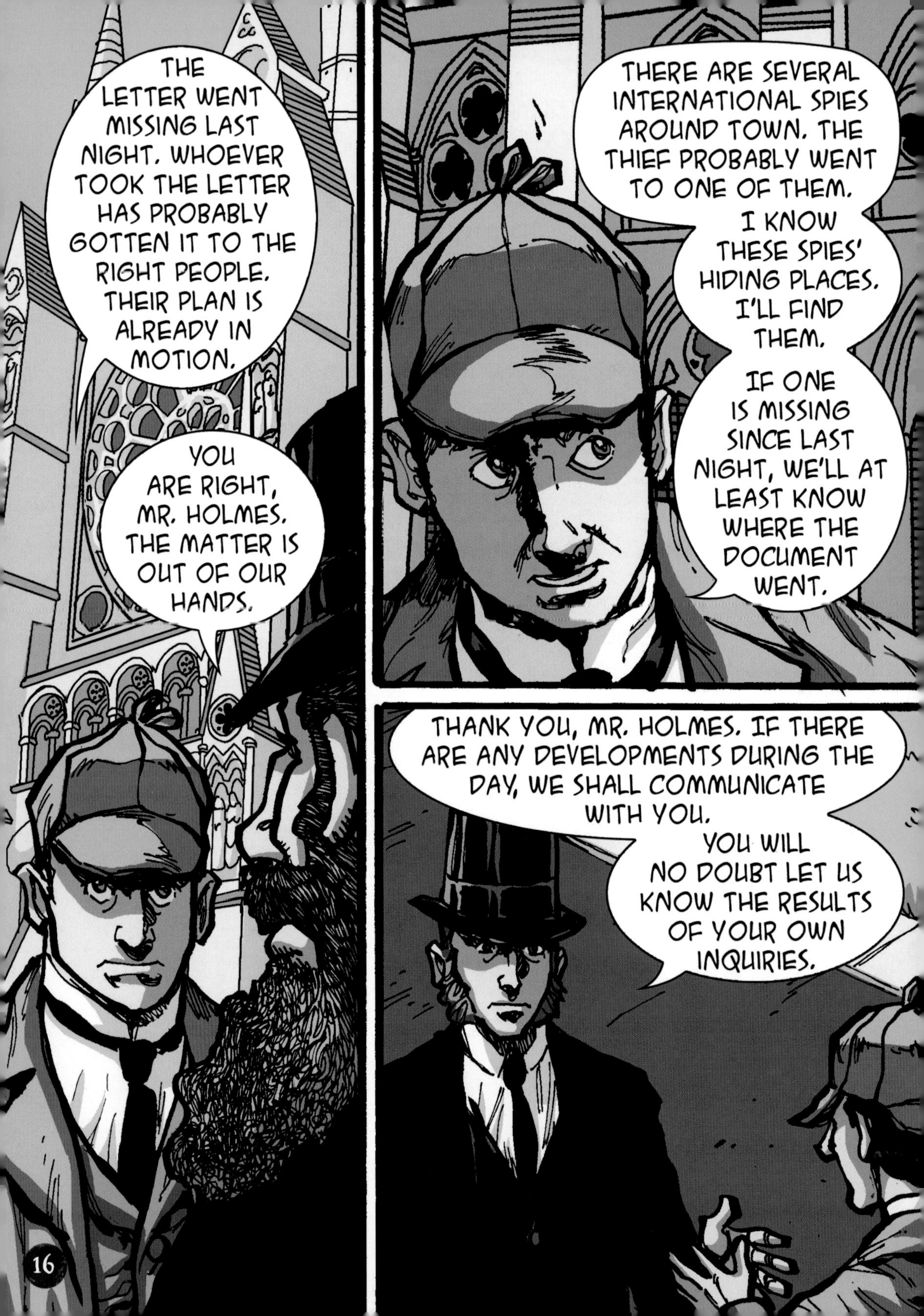
THE LETTER WENT MISSING LAST NIGHT. WHOEVER TOOK THE LETTER HAS PROBABLY GOTTEN IT TO THE RIGHT PEOPLE. THEIR PLAN IS ALREADY IN MOTION.
YOU ARE RIGHT, MR. HOLMES. THE MATTER IS OUT OF OUR HANDS.
THERE ARE SEVERAL INTERNATIONAL SPIES AROUND TOWN. THE THIEF PROBABLY WENT TO ONE OF THEM.
I KNOW THESE SPIES' HIDING PLACES. I'LL FIND THEM.
IF ONE IS MISSING SINCE LAST NIGHT, WE'LL AT LEAST KNOW WHERE THE DOCUMENT WENT.
THANK YOU, MR. HOLMES. IF THERE ARE ANY DEVELOPMENTS DURING THE DAY, WE SHALL COMMUNICATE WITH YOU.
YOU WILL NO DOUBT LET US KNOW THE RESULTS OF YOUR OWN INQUIRIES.

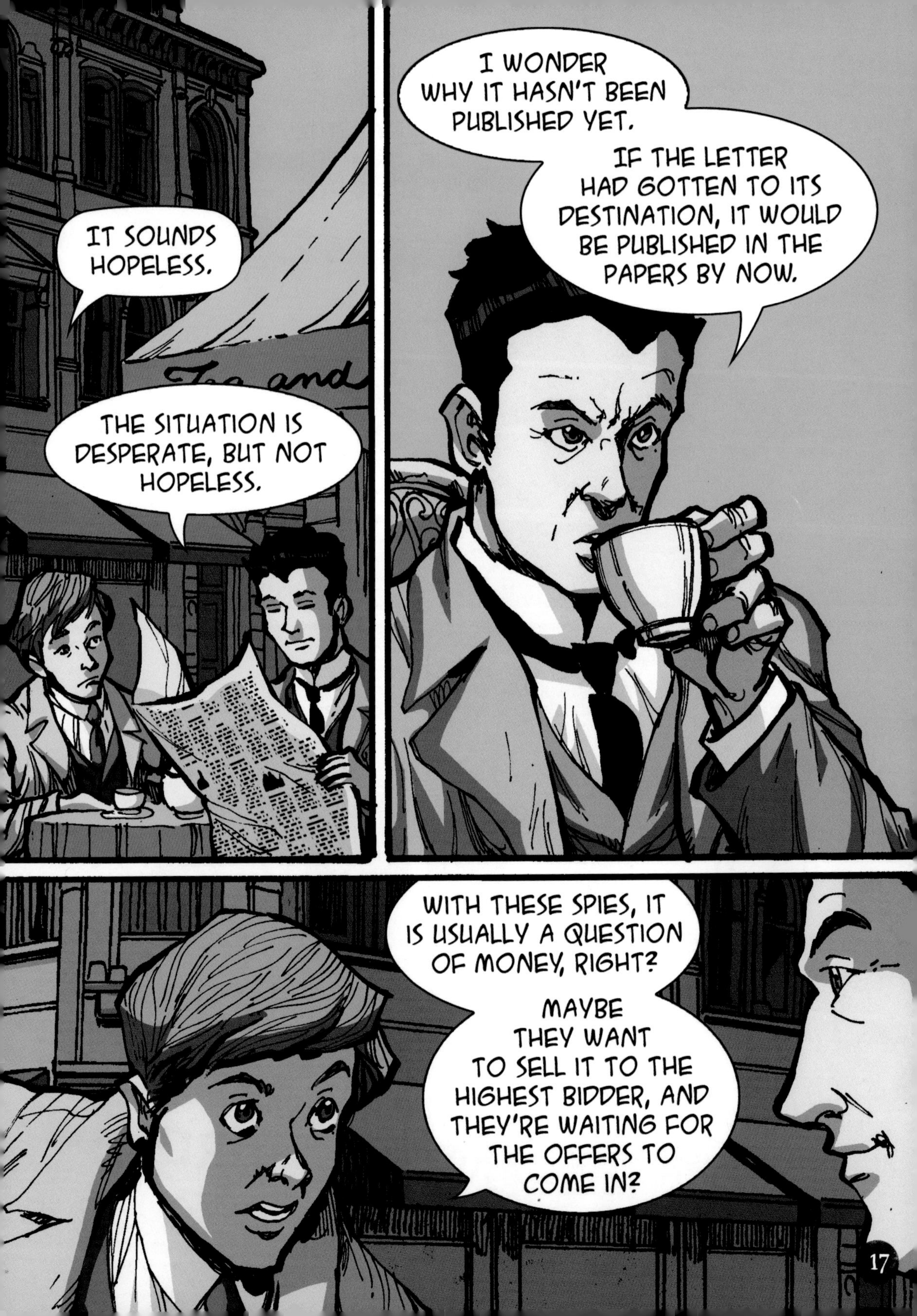
IT SOUNDS HOPELESS.
THE SITUATION IS DESPERATE, BUT NOT HOPELESS.
I WONDER WHY IT HASN'T BEEN PUBLISHED YET.
IF THE LETTER HAD GOTTEN TO ITS DESTINATION, IT WOULD BE PUBLISHED IN THE PAPERS BY NOW.
WITH THESE SPIES, IT IS USUALLY A QUESTION OF MONEY, RIGHT?
MAYBE THEY WANT TO SELL IT TO THE HIGHEST BIDDER, AND THEY'RE WAITING FOR THE OFFERS TO COME IN?

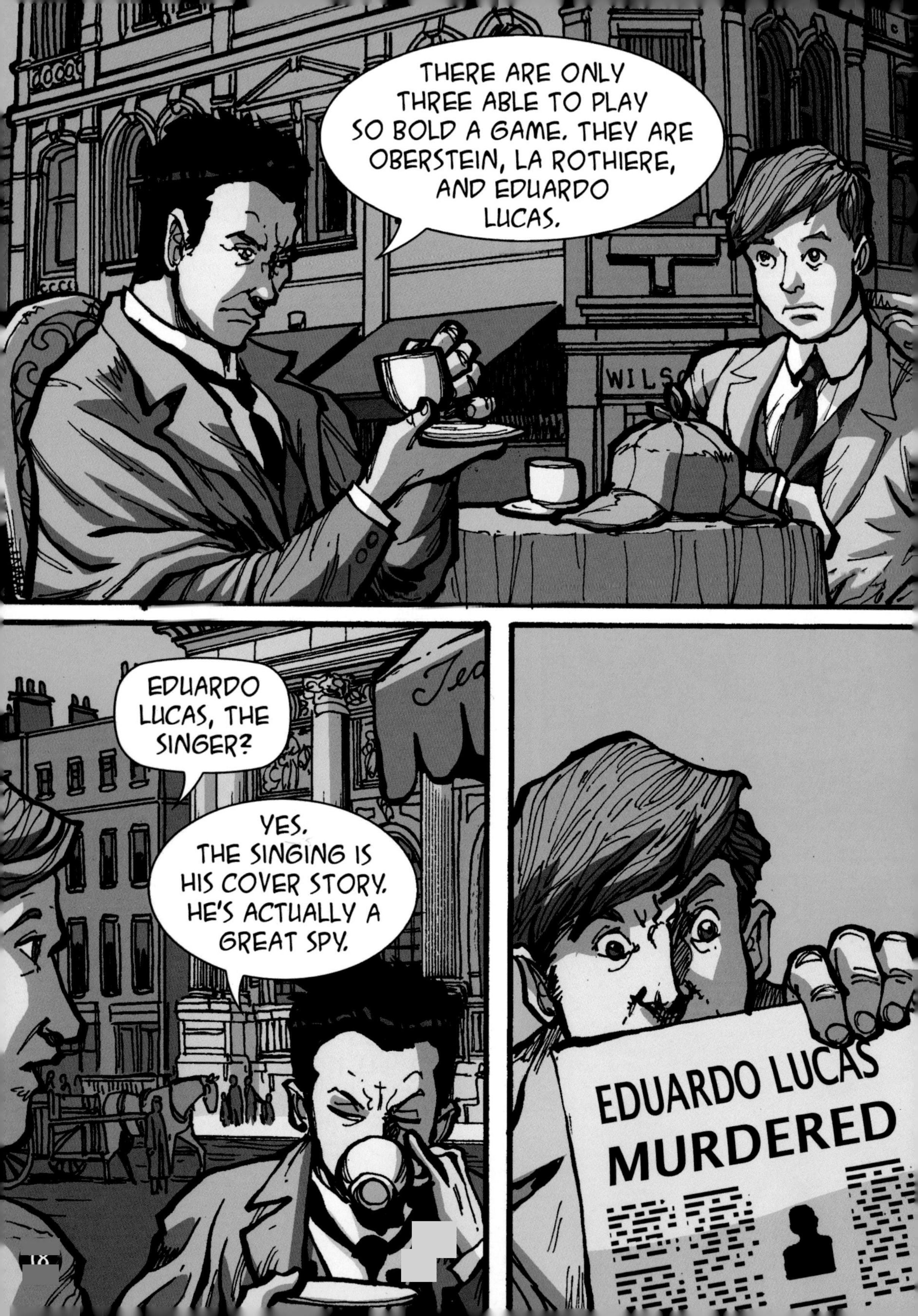
THERE ARE ONLY THREE ABLE TO PLAY SO BOLD A GAME. THEY ARE OBERSTEIN, LA ROTHIERE, AND EDUARDO LUCAS.
EDUARDO LUCAS, THE SINGER?
YES. THE SINGING IS HIS COVER STORY. HE'S ACTUALLY A GREAT SPY.
EDUARDO LUCAS
MURDERED

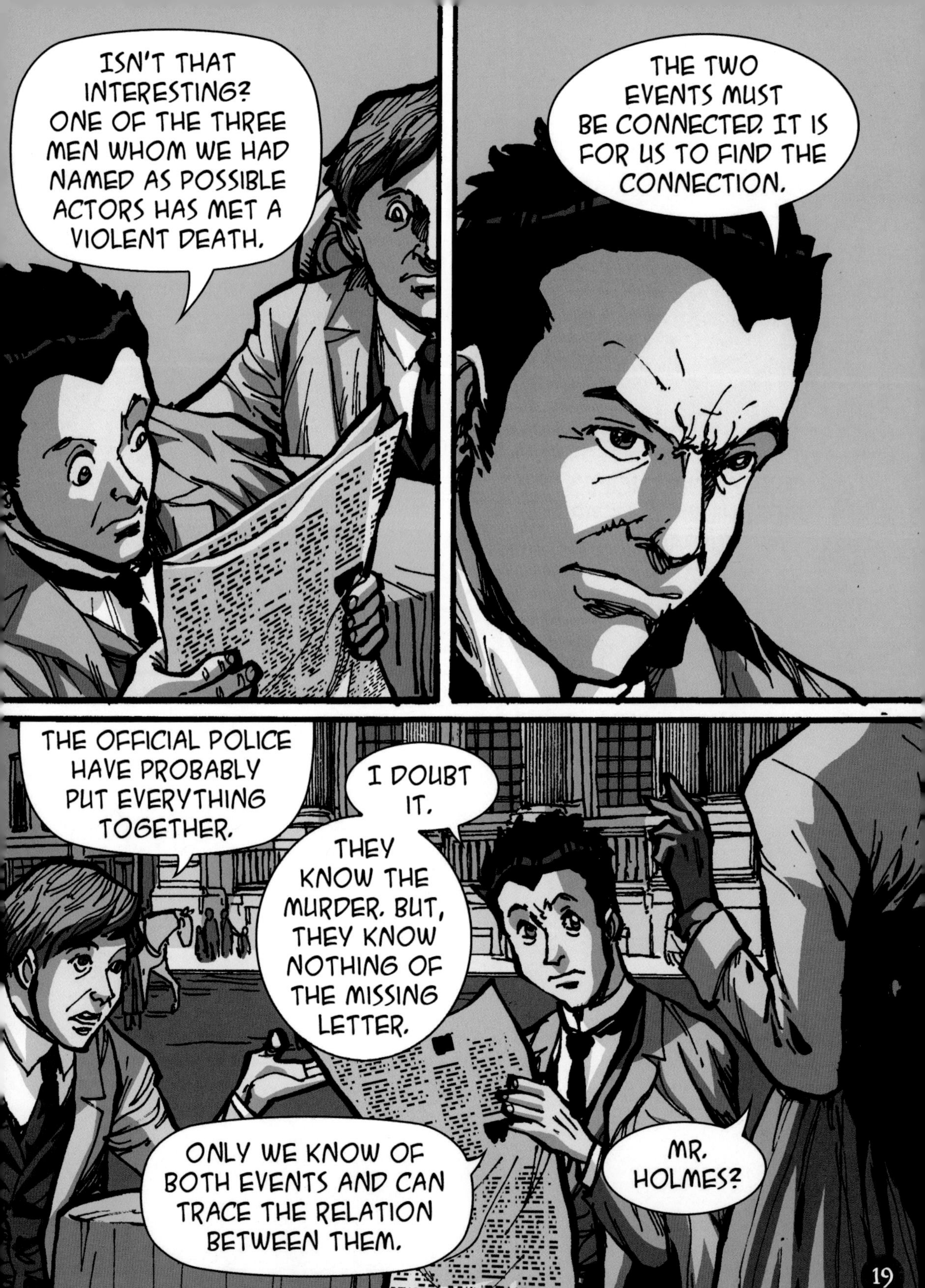
ISN'T THAT INTERESTING? ONE OF THE THREE MEN WHOM WE HAD NAMED AS POSSIBLE ACTORS HAS MET A VIOLENT DEATH.
THE TWO EVENTS MUST BE CONNECTED. IT IS FOR US TO FIND THE CONNECTION.
THE OFFICIAL POLICE HAVE PROBABLY PUT EVERYTHING TOGETHER.
I DOUBT IT.
THEY KNOW THE MURDER. BUT, THEY KNOW NOTHING OF THE MISSING LETTER.
ONLY WE KNOW OF BOTH EVENTS AND CAN TRACE THE RELATION BETWEEN THEM.
MR. HOLMES?

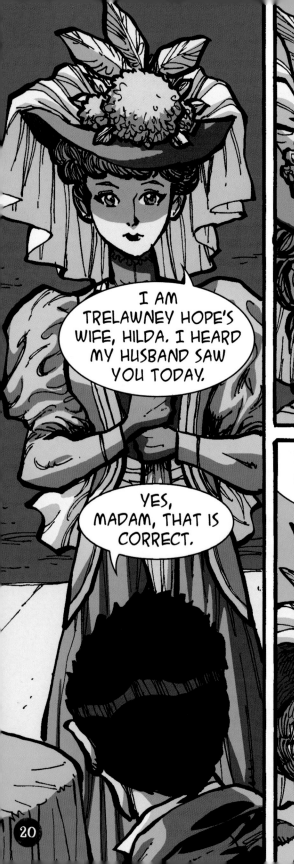

I AM TRELAWNEY HOPE'S WIFE, HILDA. I HEARD MY HUSBAND SAW YOU TODAY.

YES, MADAM, THAT IS CORRECT.

I KNOW THAT A PAPER DISAPPEARED FROM OUR HOUSE LAST NIGHT. BUT BECAUSE THE MATTER IS RELATED TO HIS JOB, MY HUSBAND REFUSES TO TELL ME WHAT WAS IN THE PAPER.

I BEG YOU, MR. HOLMES, TO TELL ME EXACTLY WHAT HAS HAPPENED AND WHAT IT WILL LEAD TO.

MADAM, WHAT YOU ASK ME IS REALLY IMPOSSIBLE. IT IS HIM WHOM YOU MUST ASK.

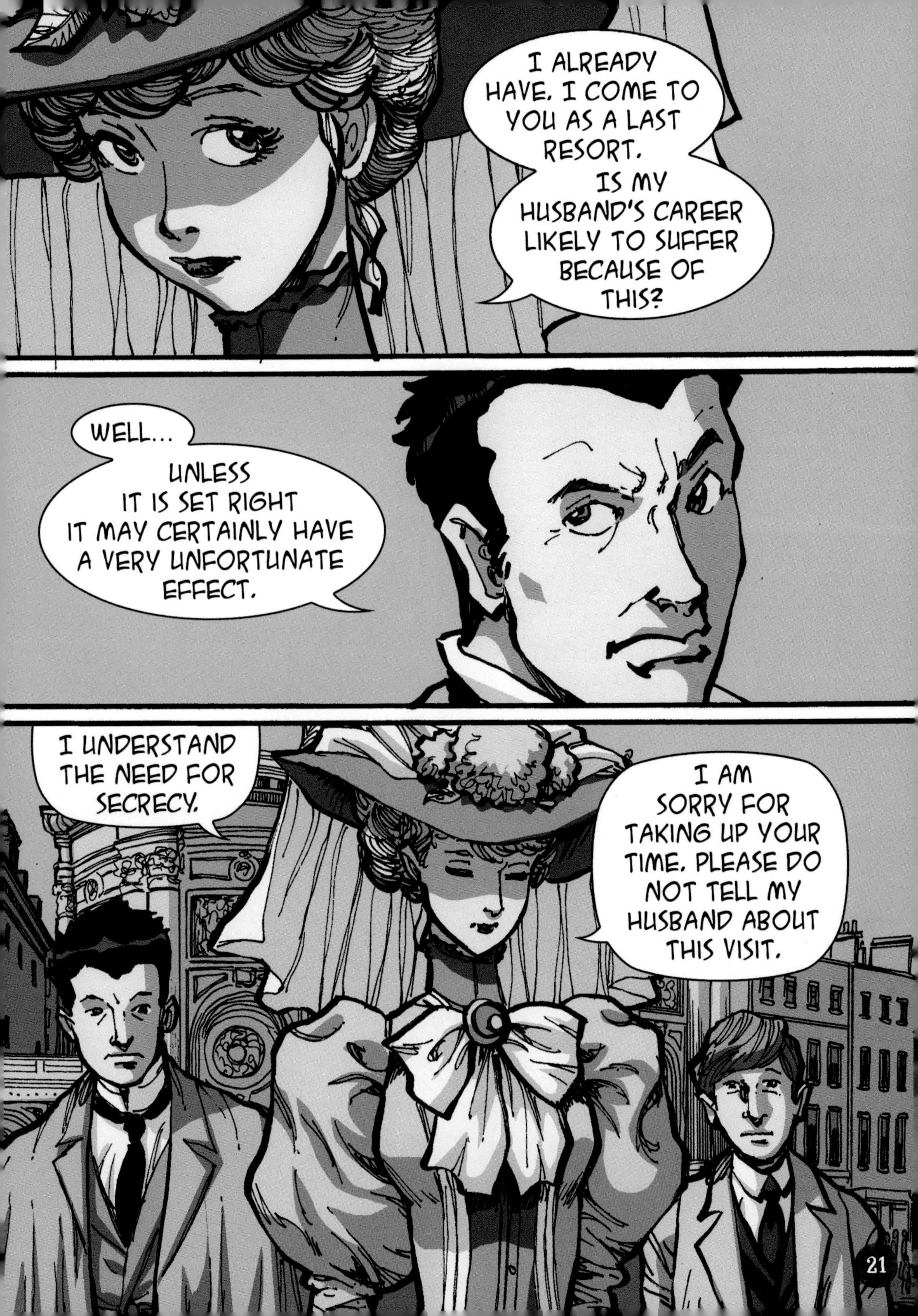
I ALREADY HAVE. I COME TO YOU AS A LAST RESORT.
IS MY HUSBAND'S CAREER LIKELY TO SUFFER BECAUSE OF THIS?
WELL...
UNLESS IT IS SET RIGHT IT MAY CERTAINLY HAVE A VERY UNFORTUNATE EFFECT.
I UNDERSTAND THE NEED FOR SECRECY.
I AM SORRY FOR TAKING UP YOUR TIME. PLEASE DO NOT TELL MY HUSBAND ABOUT THIS VISIT.

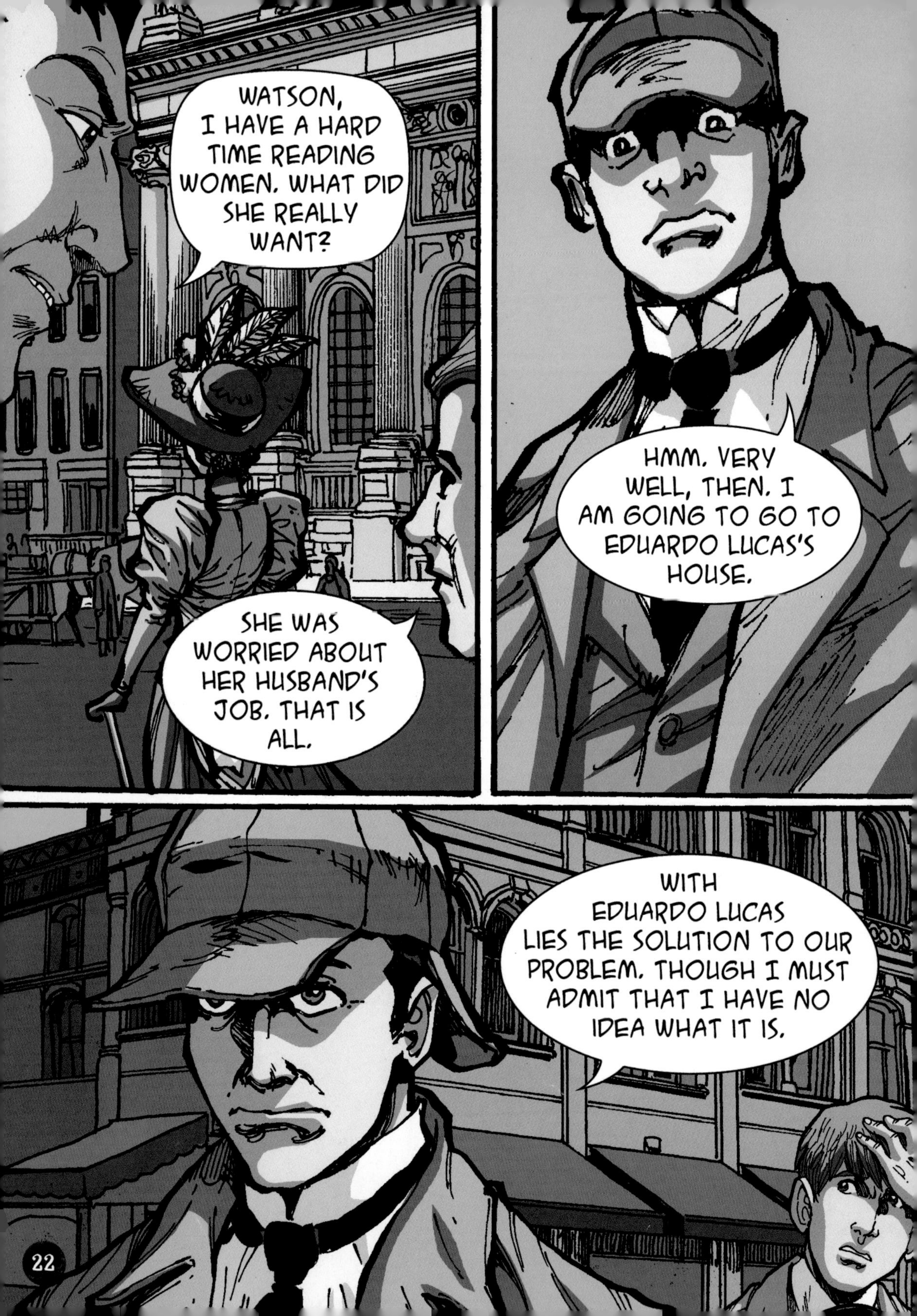
WATSON, I HAVE A HARD TIME READING WOMEN. WHAT DID SHE REALLY WANT?
SHE WAS WORRIED ABOUT HER HUSBAND'S JOB. THAT IS ALL.
HMM. VERY WELL, THEN. I AM GOING TO GO TO EDUARDO LUCAS'S HOUSE.
WITH EDUARDO LUCAS LIES THE SOLUTION TO OUR PROBLEM. THOUGH I MUST ADMIT THAT I HAVE NO IDEA WHAT IT IS.

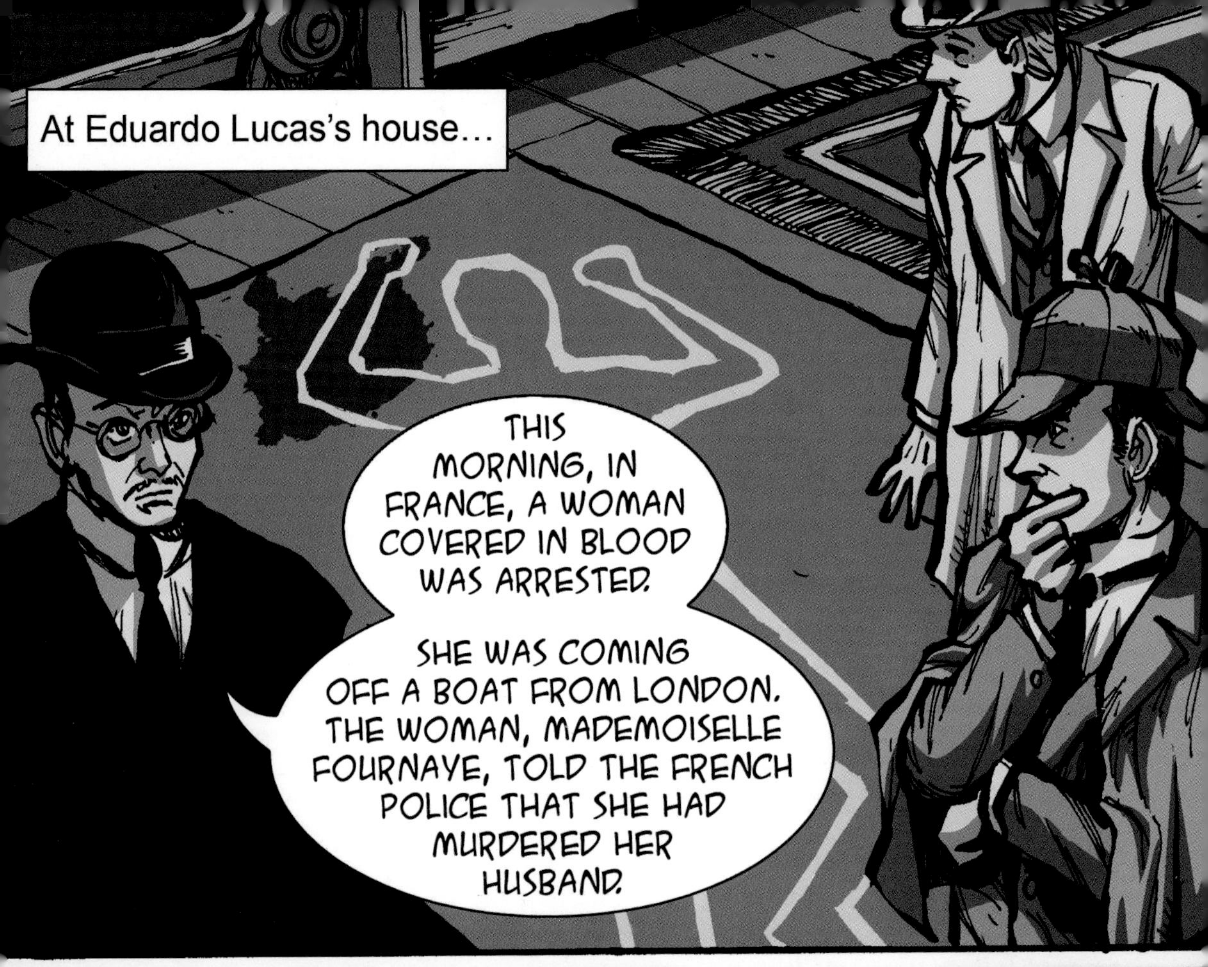
At Eduardo Lucas's house…
THIS MORNING, IN FRANCE, A WOMAN COVERED IN BLOOD WAS ARRESTED.
SHE WAS COMING OFF A BOAT FROM LONDON. THE WOMAN, MADEMOISELLE FOURNAYE, TOLD THE FRENCH POLICE THAT SHE HAD MURDERED HER HUSBAND.

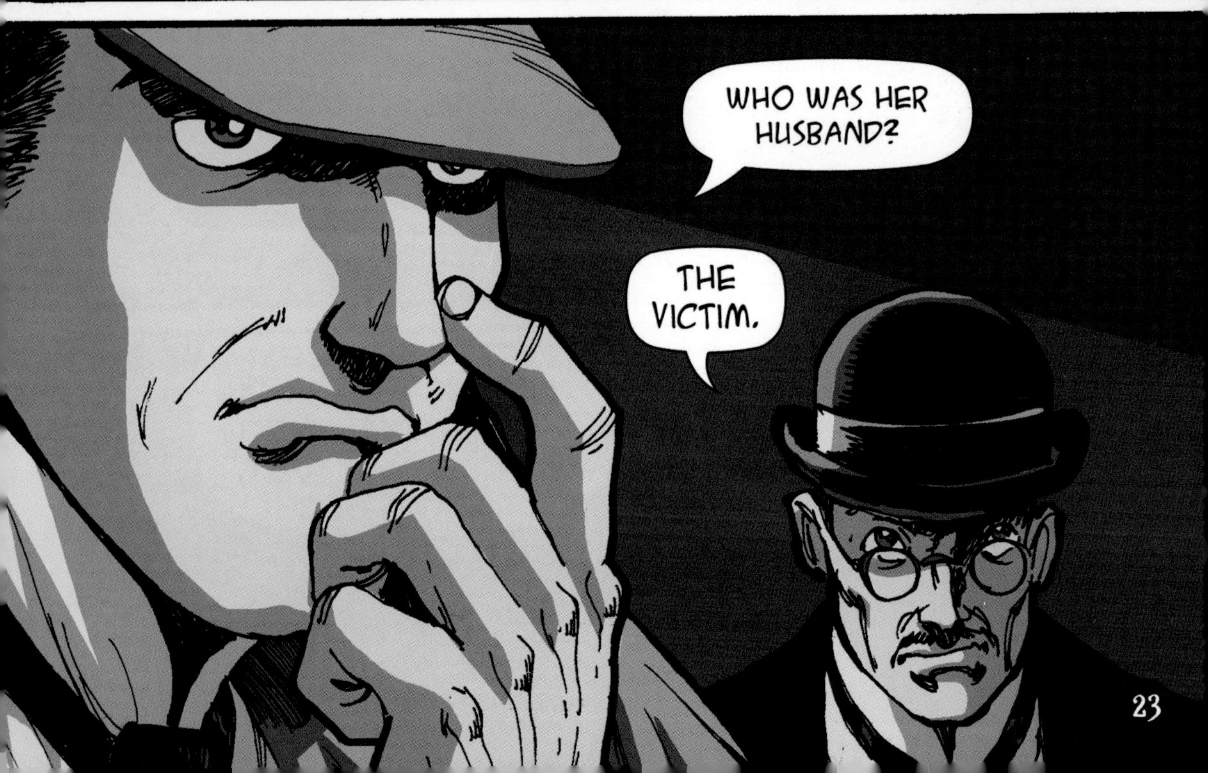
WHO WAS HER HUSBAND?
THE VICTIM.

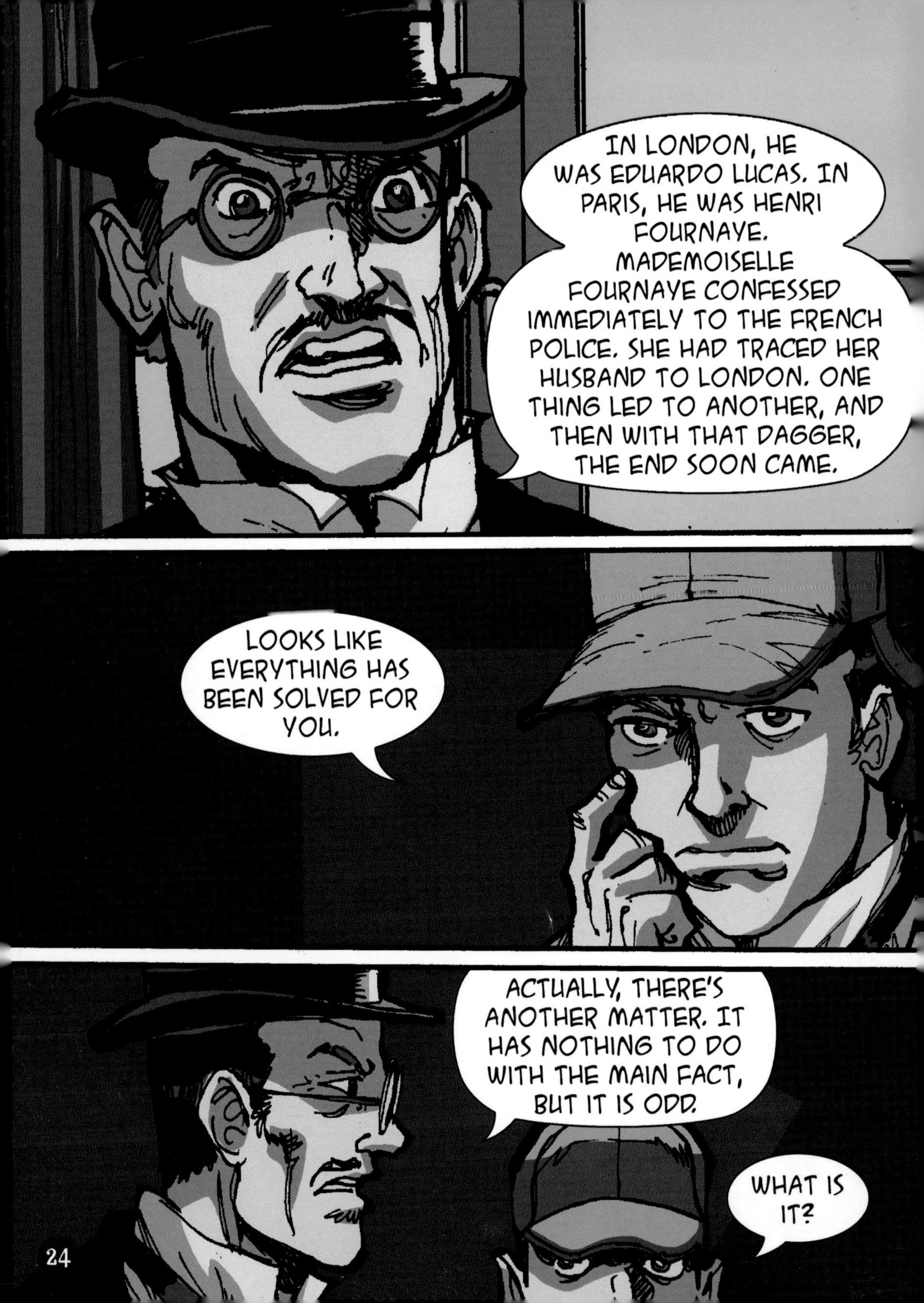
IN LONDON, HE WAS EDUARDO LUCAS. IN PARIS, HE WAS HENRI FOURNAYE. MADEMOISELLE FOURNAYE CONFESSED IMMEDIATELY TO THE FRENCH POLICE. SHE HAD TRACED HER HUSBAND TO LONDON. ONE THING LED TO ANOTHER, AND THEN WITH THAT DAGGER, THE END SOON CAME.
LOOKS LIKE EVERYTHING HAS BEEN SOLVED FOR YOU.
ACTUALLY, THERE'S ANOTHER MATTER. IT HAS NOTHING TO DO WITH THE MAIN FACT, BUT IT IS ODD.
WHAT IS IT?

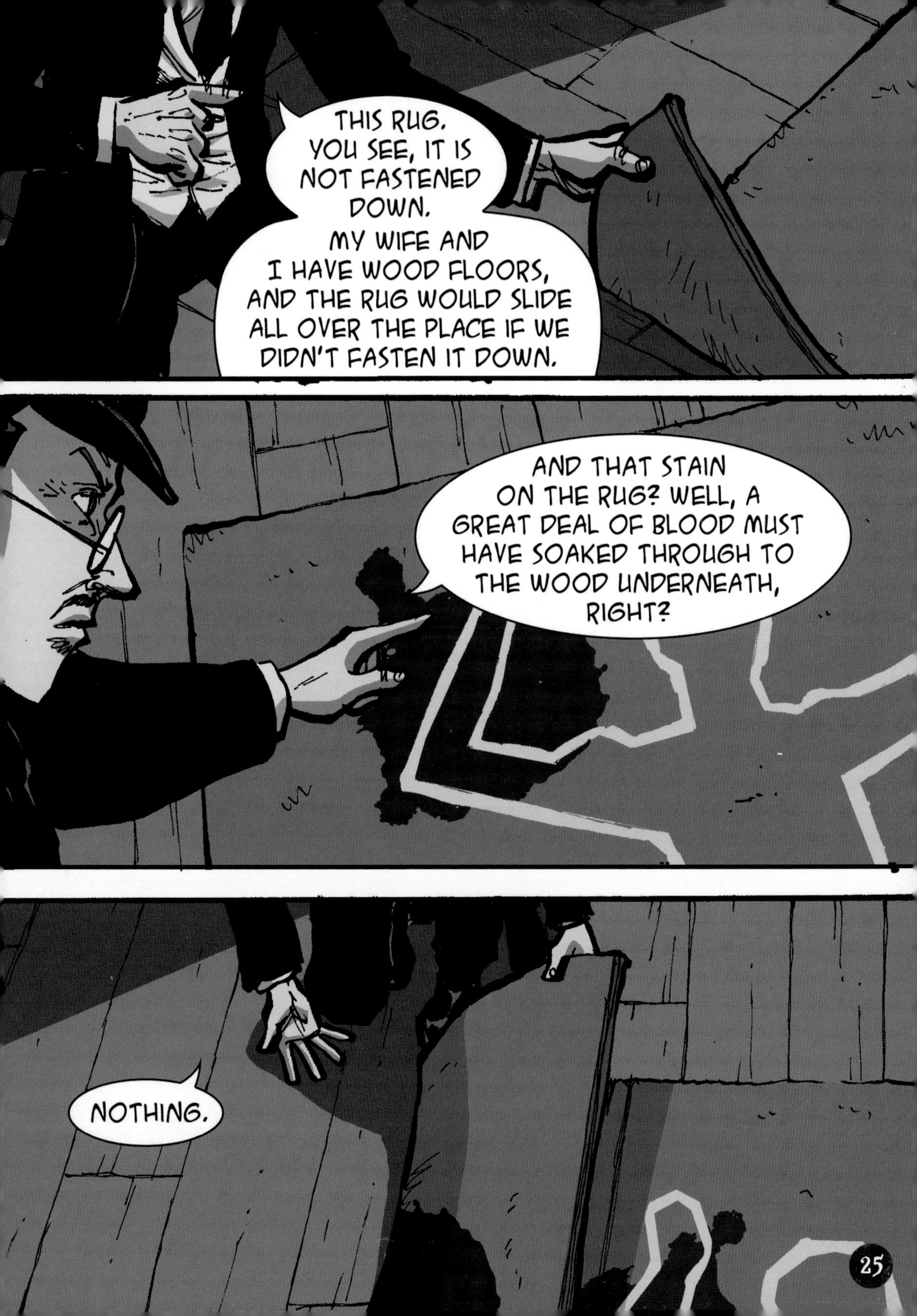
THIS RUG. YOU SEE, IT IS NOT FASTENED DOWN.
MY WIFE AND I HAVE WOOD FLOORS, AND THE RUG WOULD SLIDE ALL OVER THE PLACE IF WE DIDN'T FASTEN IT DOWN.
AND THAT STAIN ON THE RUG? WELL, A GREAT DEAL OF BLOOD MUST HAVE SOAKED THROUGH TO THE WOOD UNDERNEATH, RIGHT?
NOTHING.

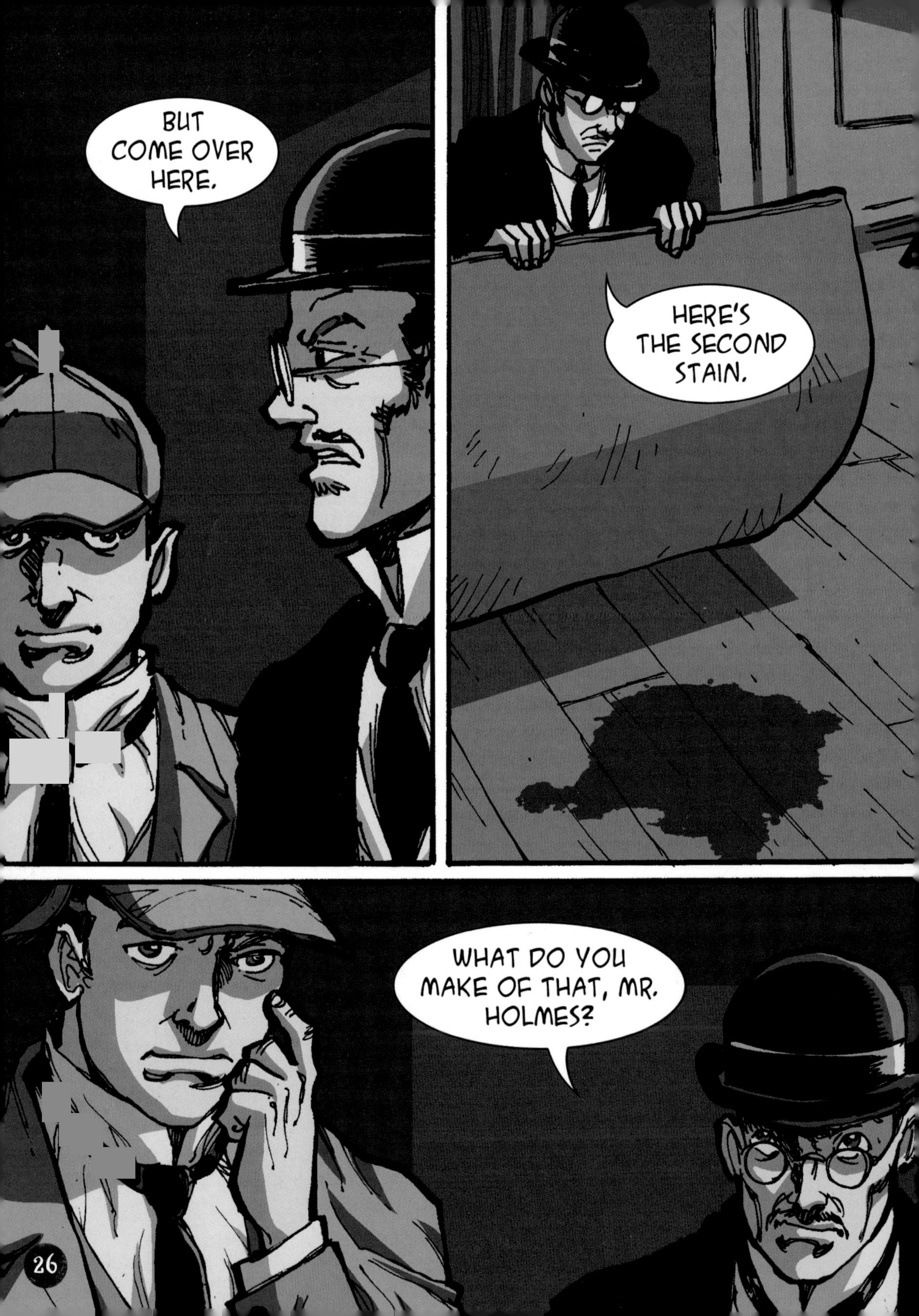
BUT COME OVER HERE.
HERE'S THE SECOND STAIN.
WHAT DO YOU MAKE OF THAT, MR. HOLMES?

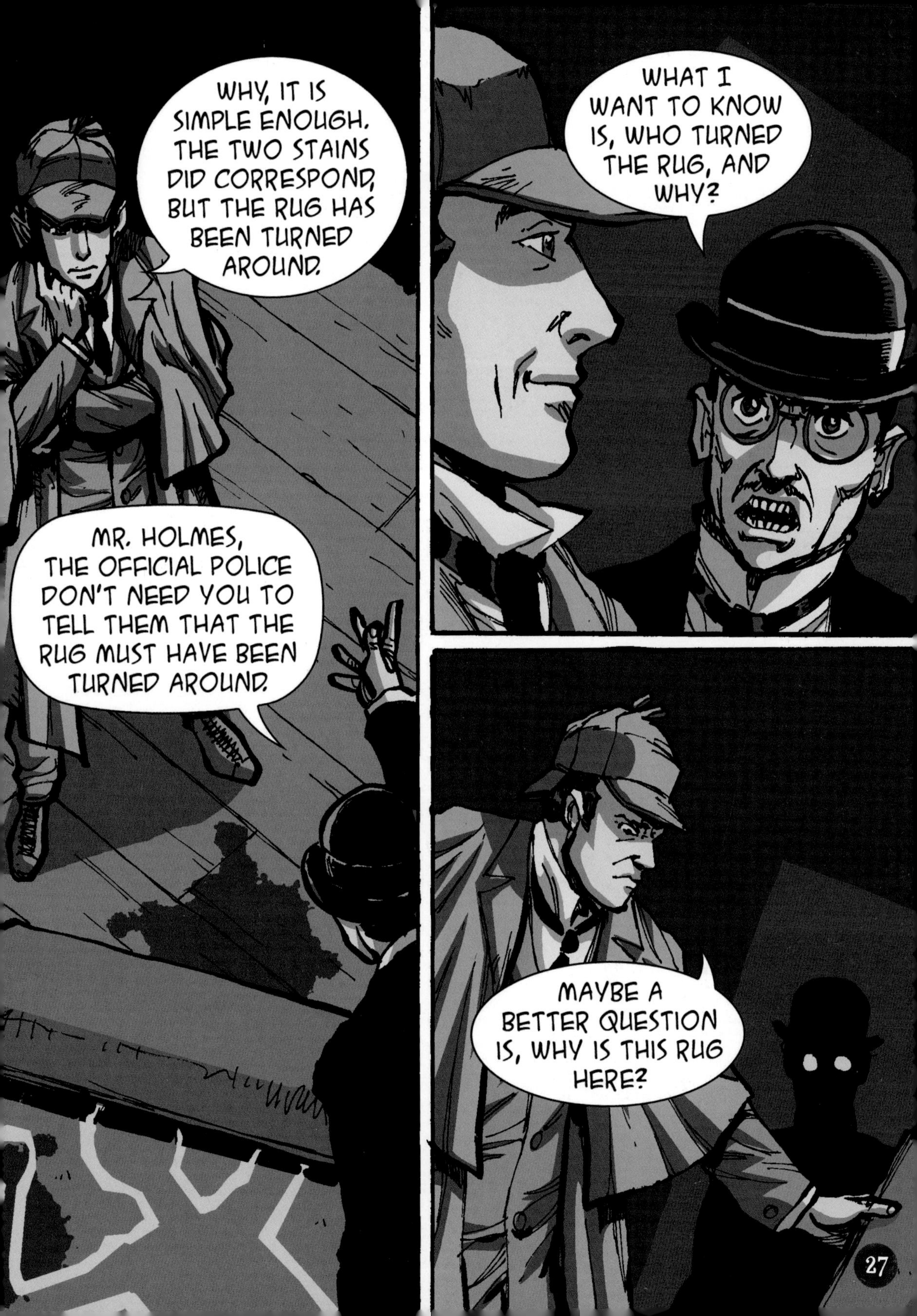
WHY, IT IS SIMPLE ENOUGH. THE TWO STAINS DID CORRESPOND, BUT THE RUG HAS BEEN TURNED AROUND.
MR. HOLMES, THE OFFICIAL POLICE DON'T NEED YOU TO TELL THEM THAT THE RUG MUST HAVE BEEN TURNED AROUND.
WHAT I WANT TO KNOW IS, WHO TURNED THE RUG, AND WHY?
MAYBE A BETTER QUESTION IS, WHY IS THIS RUG HERE?

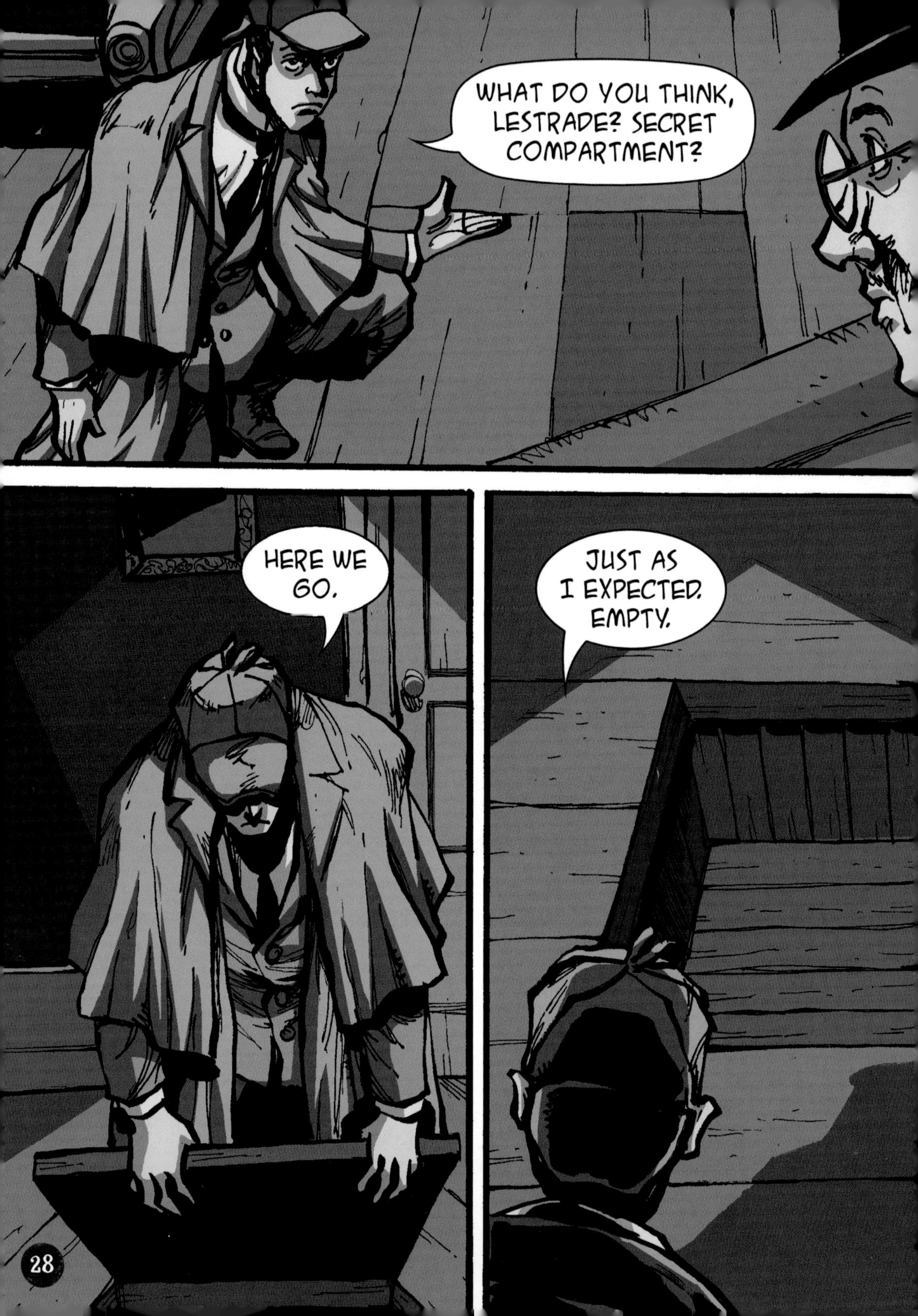
WHAT DO YOU THINK, LESTRADE? SECRET COMPARTMENT?
HERE WE GO.
JUST AS I EXPECTED. EMPTY.

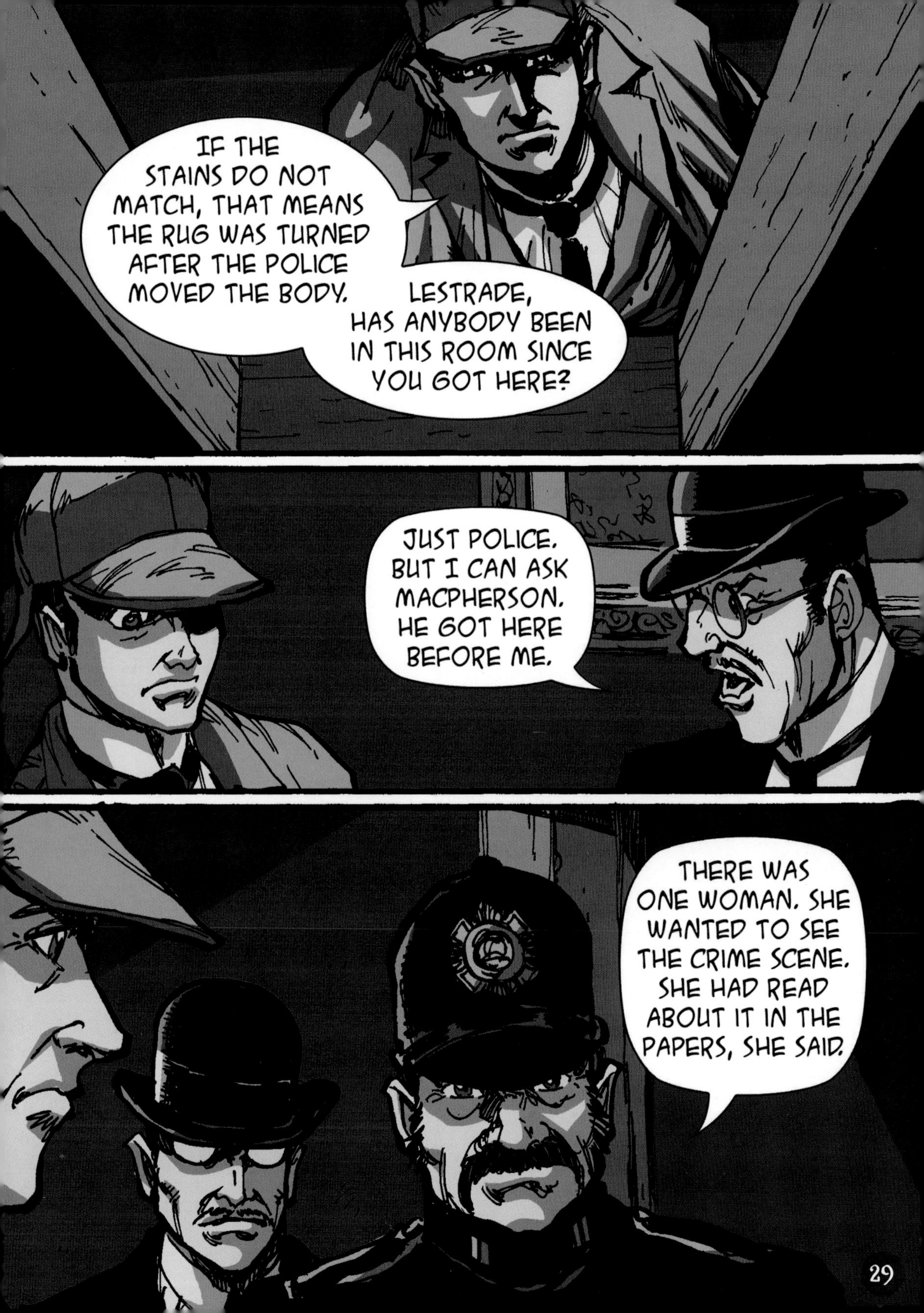
IF THE STAINS DO NOT MATCH, THAT MEANS THE RUG WAS TURNED AFTER THE POLICE MOVED THE BODY.
LESTRADE, HAS ANYBODY BEEN IN THIS ROOM SINCE YOU GOT HERE?
JUST POLICE. BUT I CAN ASK MACPHERSON. HE GOT HERE BEFORE ME.
THERE WAS ONE WOMAN. SHE WANTED TO SEE THE CRIME SCENE. SHE HAD READ ABOUT IT IN THE PAPERS, SHE SAID.

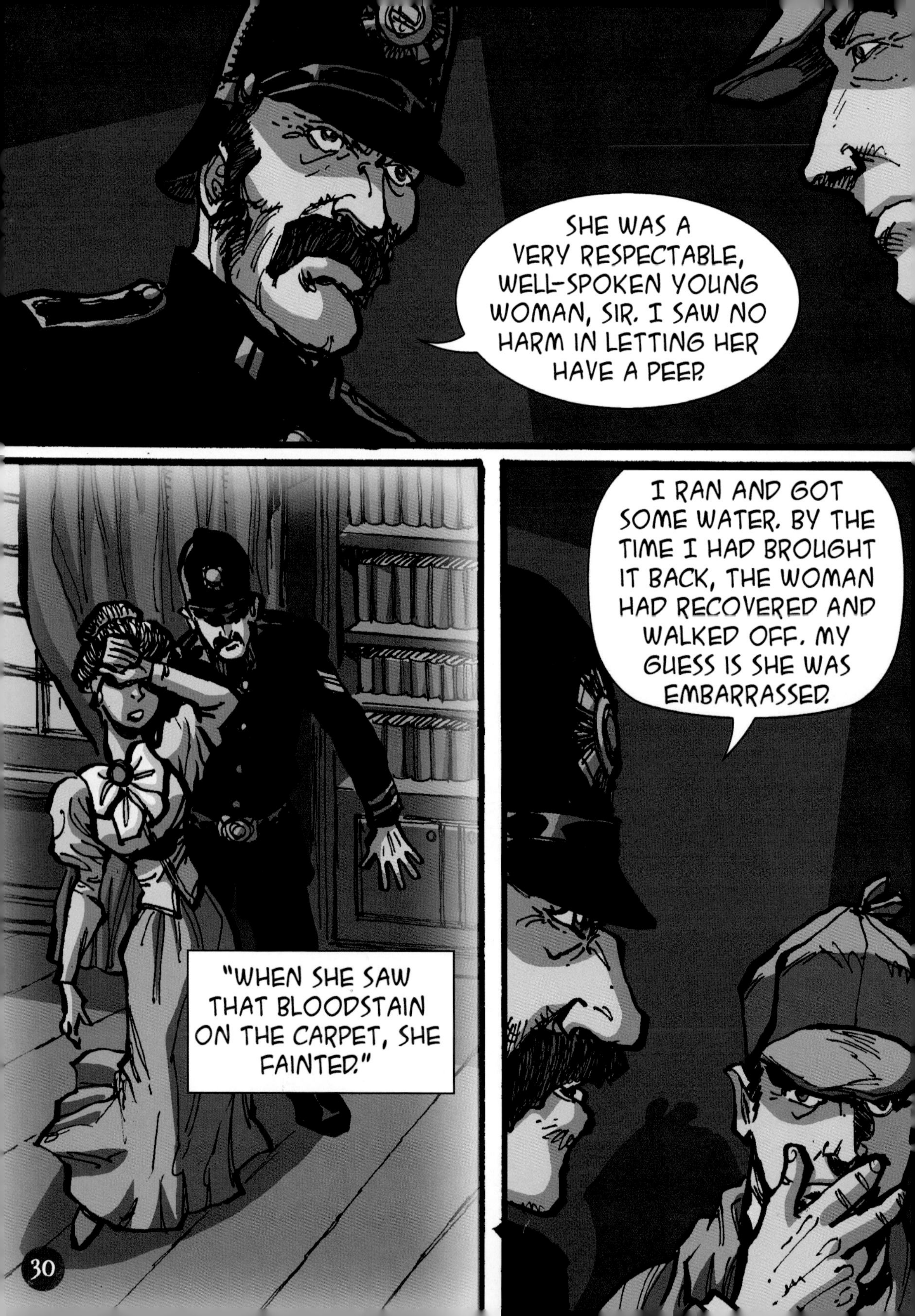
SHE WAS A VERY RESPECTABLE, WELL-SPOKEN YOUNG WOMAN, SIR. I SAW NO HARM IN LETTING HER HAVE A PEEP.
"WHEN SHE SAW THAT BLOODSTAIN ON THE CARPET, SHE FAINTED."
I RAN AND GOT SOME WATER. BY THE TIME I HAD BROUGHT IT BACK, THE WOMAN HAD RECOVERED AND WALKED OFF. MY GUESS IS SHE WAS EMBARRASSED.

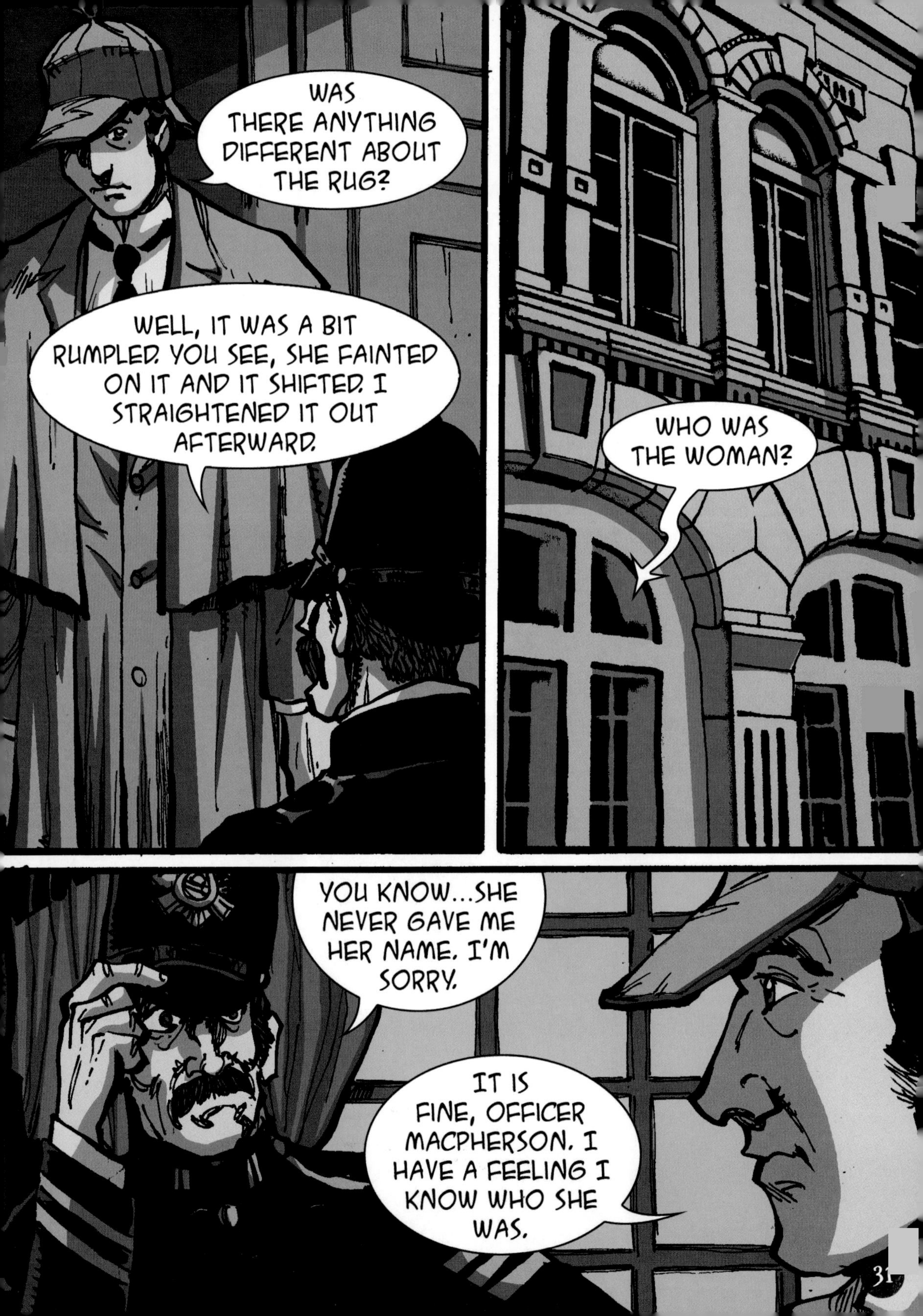
WAS THERE ANYTHING DIFFERENT ABOUT THE RUG?
WELL, IT WAS A BIT RUMPLED. YOU SEE, SHE FAINTED ON IT AND IT SHIFTED. I STRAIGHTENED IT OUT AFTERWARD.
WHO WAS THE WOMAN?
YOU KNOW...SHE NEVER GAVE ME HER NAME. I'M SORRY.
IT IS FINE, OFFICER MACPHERSON. I HAVE A FEELING I KNOW WHO SHE WAS.

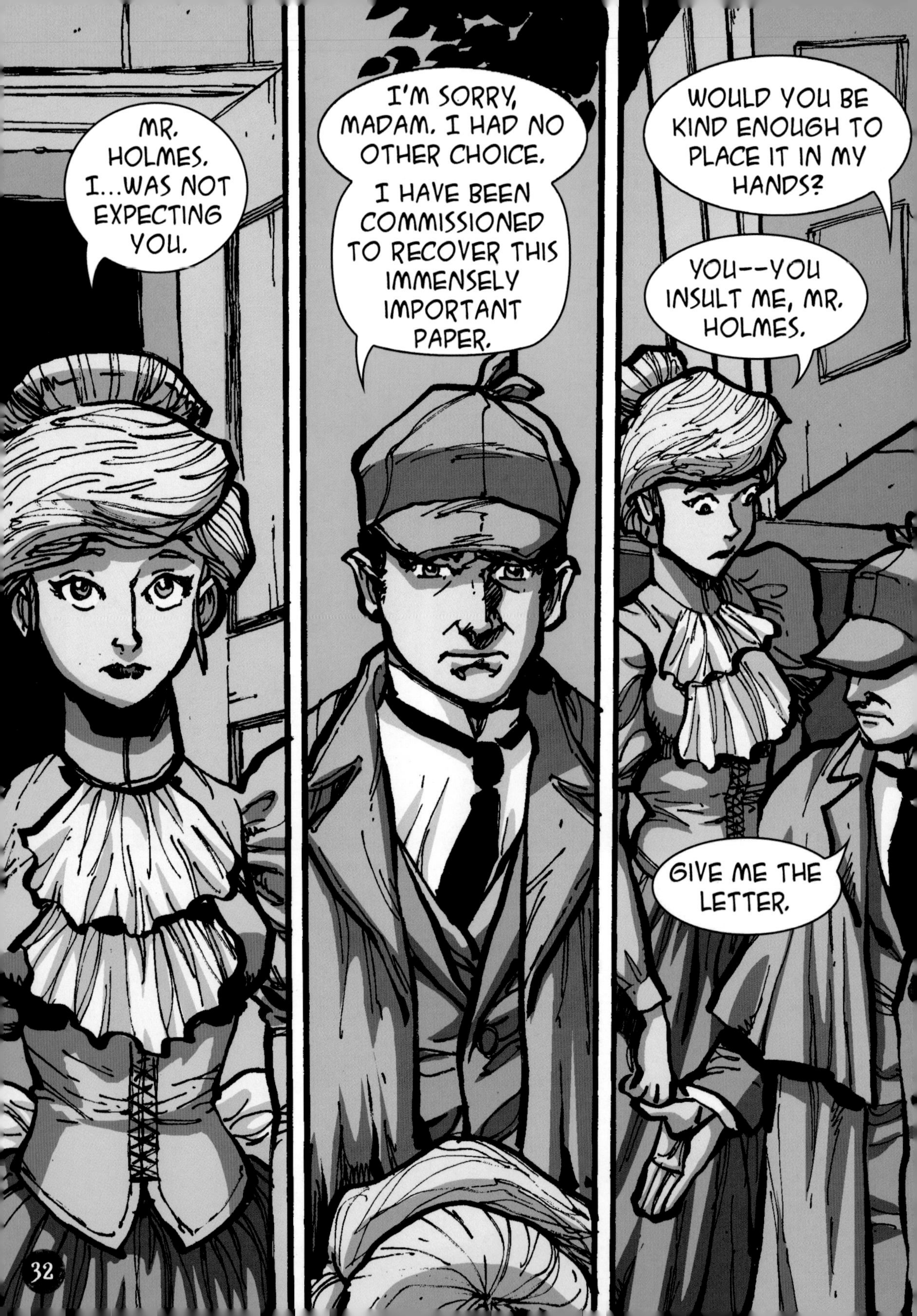
MR. HOLMES. I...WAS NOT EXPECTING YOU.
I'M SORRY, MADAM. I HAD NO OTHER CHOICE.
I HAVE BEEN COMMISSIONED TO RECOVER THIS IMMENSELY IMPORTANT PAPER.
WOULD YOU BE KIND ENOUGH TO PLACE IT IN MY HANDS?
YOU--YOU INSULT ME, MR. HOLMES.
GIVE ME THE LETTER.

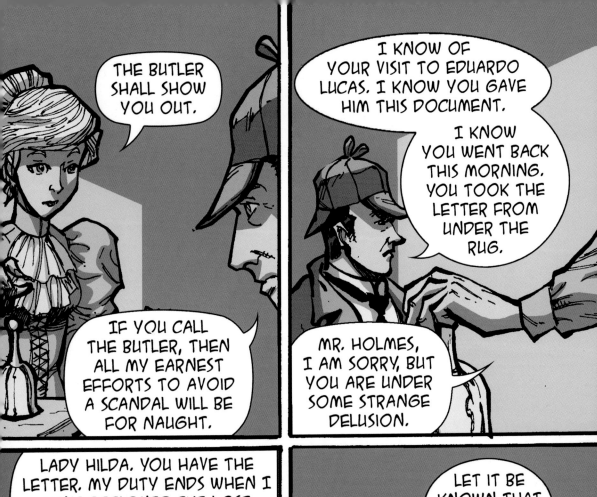

THE BUTLER SHALL SHOW YOU OUT.

I KNOW OF YOUR VISIT TO EDUARDO LUCAS. I KNOW YOU GAVE HIM THIS DOCUMENT.

I KNOW YOU WENT BACK THIS MORNING. YOU TOOK THE LETTER FROM UNDER THE RUG.

IF YOU CALL THE BUTLER, THEN ALL MY EARNEST EFFORTS TO AVOID A SCANDAL WILL BE FOR NAUGHT.

MR. HOLMES, I AM SORRY, BUT YOU ARE UNDER SOME STRANGE DELUSION.

LADY HILDA. YOU HAVE THE LETTER. MY DUTY ENDS WHEN I HAVE RETURNED THE LOST LETTER TO YOUR HUSBAND. I HAVE NO DESIRE TO BRING TROUBLE TO YOU.

I DO NOT KNOW WHAT YOU ARE TALKING ABOUT.

LET IT BE KNOWN THAT I TRIED MY BEST.

33

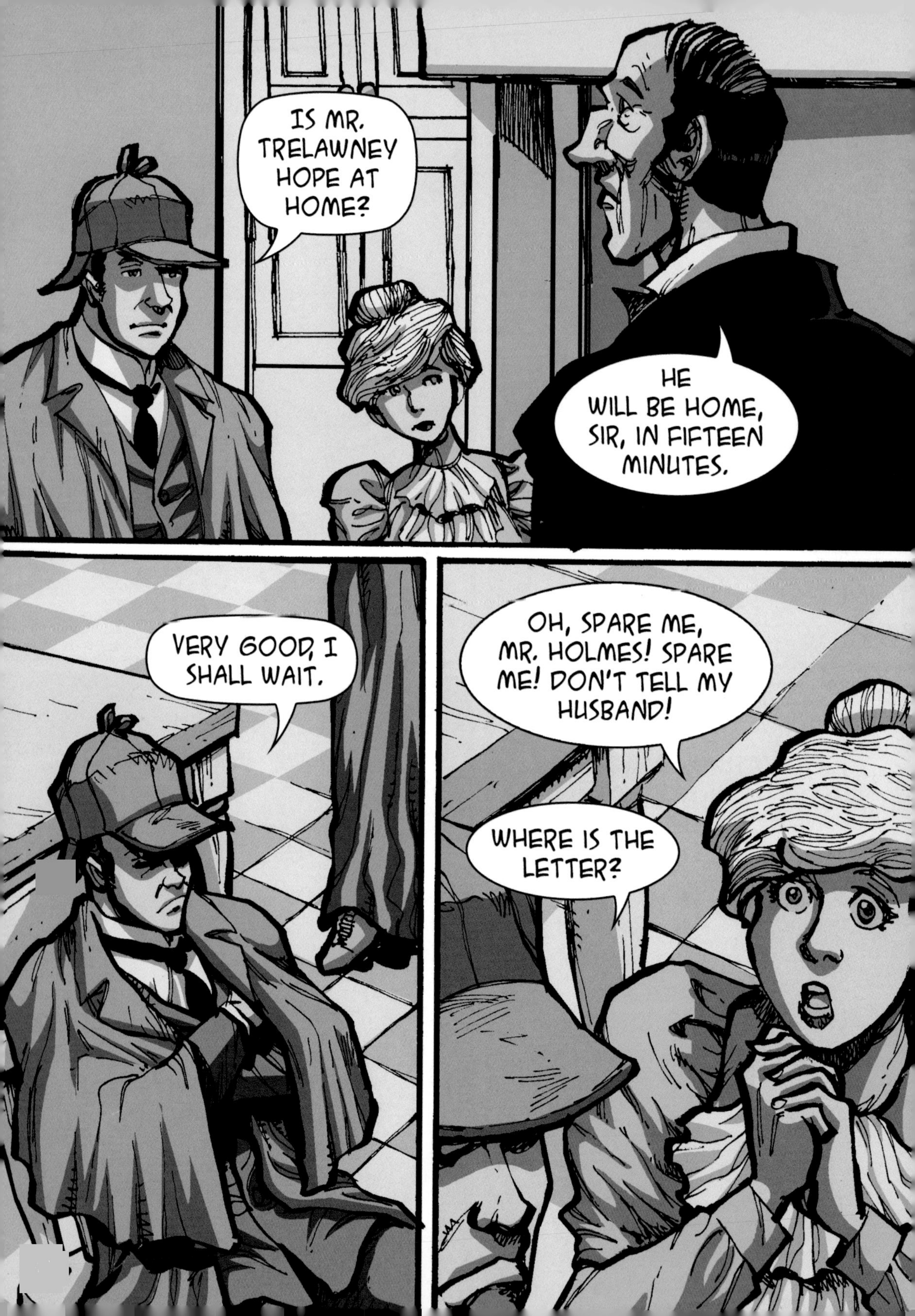

IS MR. TRELAWNEY HOPE AT HOME?
HE WILL BE HOME, SIR, IN FIFTEEN MINUTES.
VERY GOOD, I SHALL WAIT.
OH, SPARE ME, MR. HOLMES! SPARE ME! DON'T TELL MY HUSBAND!
WHERE IS THE LETTER?

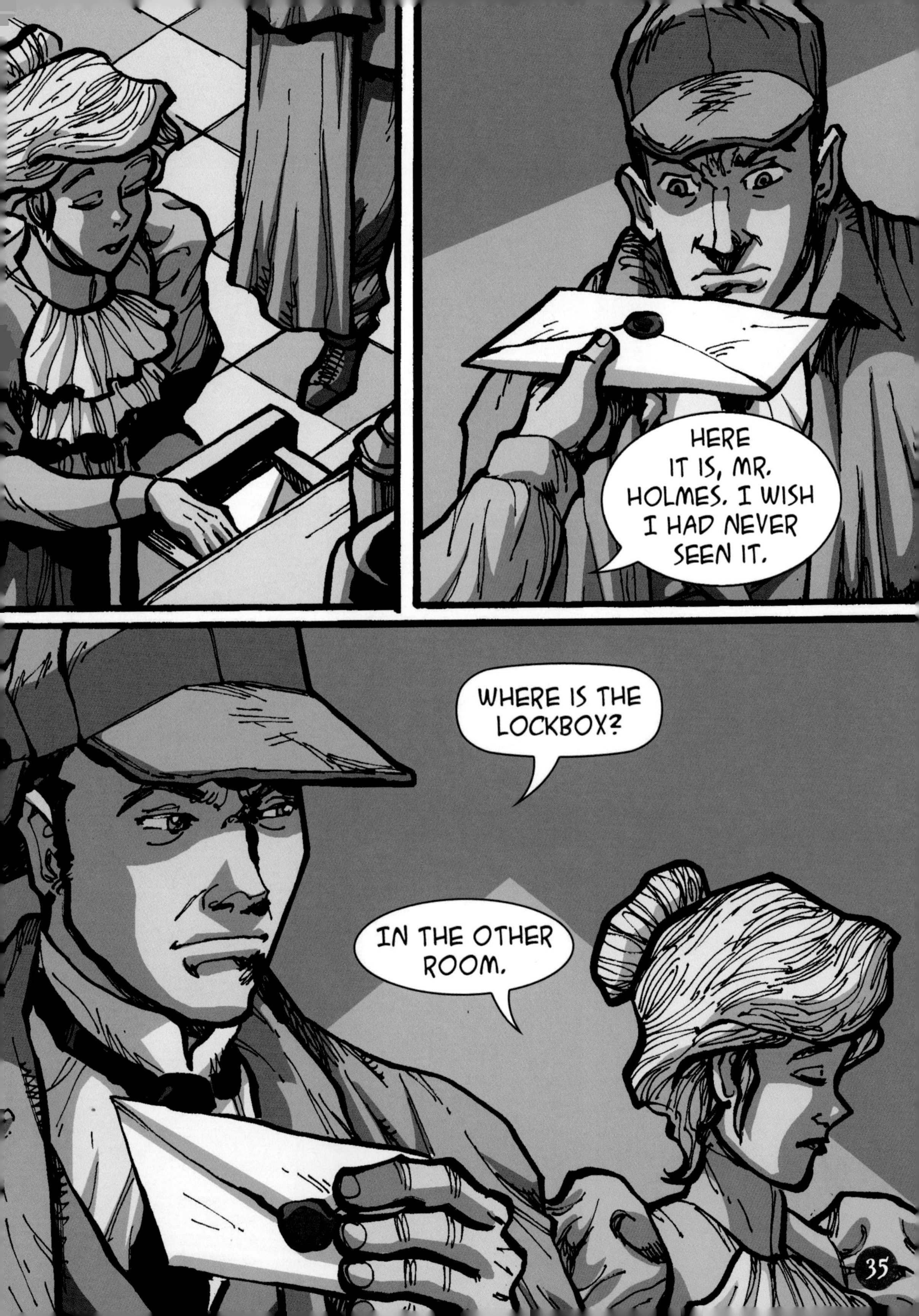
HERE IT IS, MR. HOLMES. I WISH I HAD NEVER SEEN IT.
WHERE IS THE LOCKBOX?
IN THE OTHER ROOM.

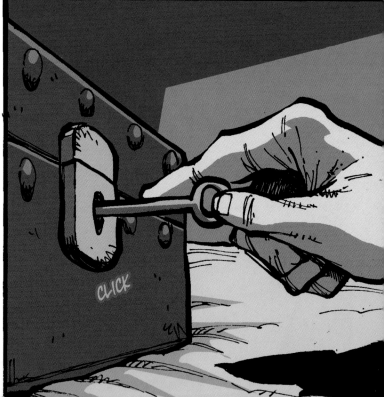

CLICK

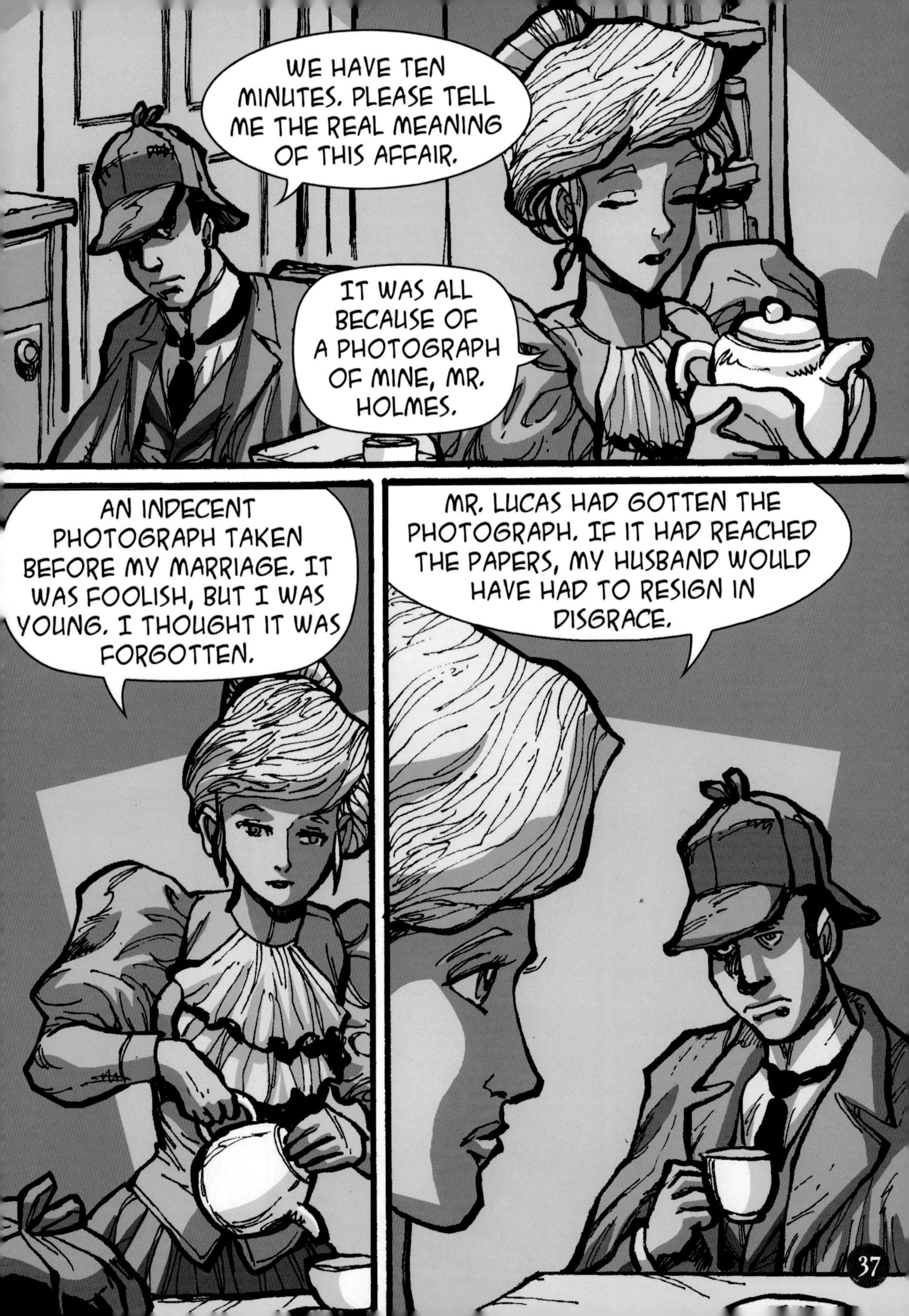
WE HAVE TEN MINUTES. PLEASE TELL ME THE REAL MEANING OF THIS AFFAIR.
IT WAS ALL BECAUSE OF A PHOTOGRAPH OF MINE, MR. HOLMES.
AN INDECENT PHOTOGRAPH TAKEN BEFORE MY MARRIAGE. IT WAS FOOLISH, BUT I WAS YOUNG. I THOUGHT IT WAS FORGOTTEN.
MR. LUCAS HAD GOTTEN THE PHOTOGRAPH. IF IT HAD REACHED THE PAPERS, MY HUSBAND WOULD HAVE HAD TO RESIGN IN DISGRACE.

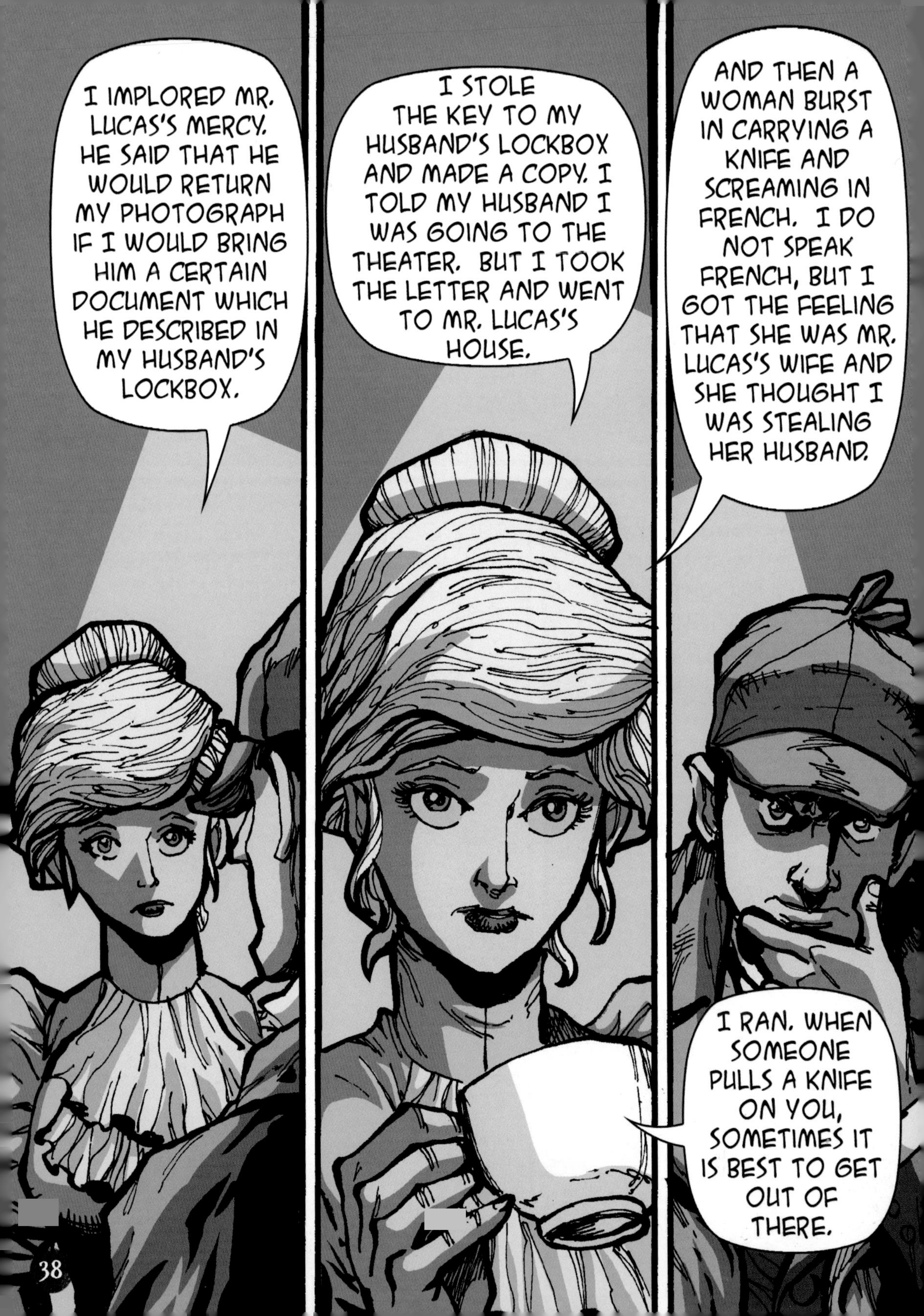
I IMPLORED MR. LUCAS'S MERCY. HE SAID THAT HE WOULD RETURN MY PHOTOGRAPH IF I WOULD BRING HIM A CERTAIN DOCUMENT WHICH HE DESCRIBED IN MY HUSBAND'S LOCKBOX.
I STOLE THE KEY TO MY HUSBAND'S LOCKBOX AND MADE A COPY. I TOLD MY HUSBAND I WAS GOING TO THE THEATER. BUT I TOOK THE LETTER AND WENT TO MR. LUCAS'S HOUSE.
AND THEN A WOMAN BURST IN CARRYING A KNIFE AND SCREAMING IN FRENCH. I DO NOT SPEAK FRENCH, BUT I GOT THE FEELING THAT SHE WAS MR. LUCAS'S WIFE AND SHE THOUGHT I WAS STEALING HER HUSBAND.
I RAN. WHEN SOMEONE PULLS A KNIFE ON YOU, SOMETIMES IT IS BEST TO GET OUT OF THERE.

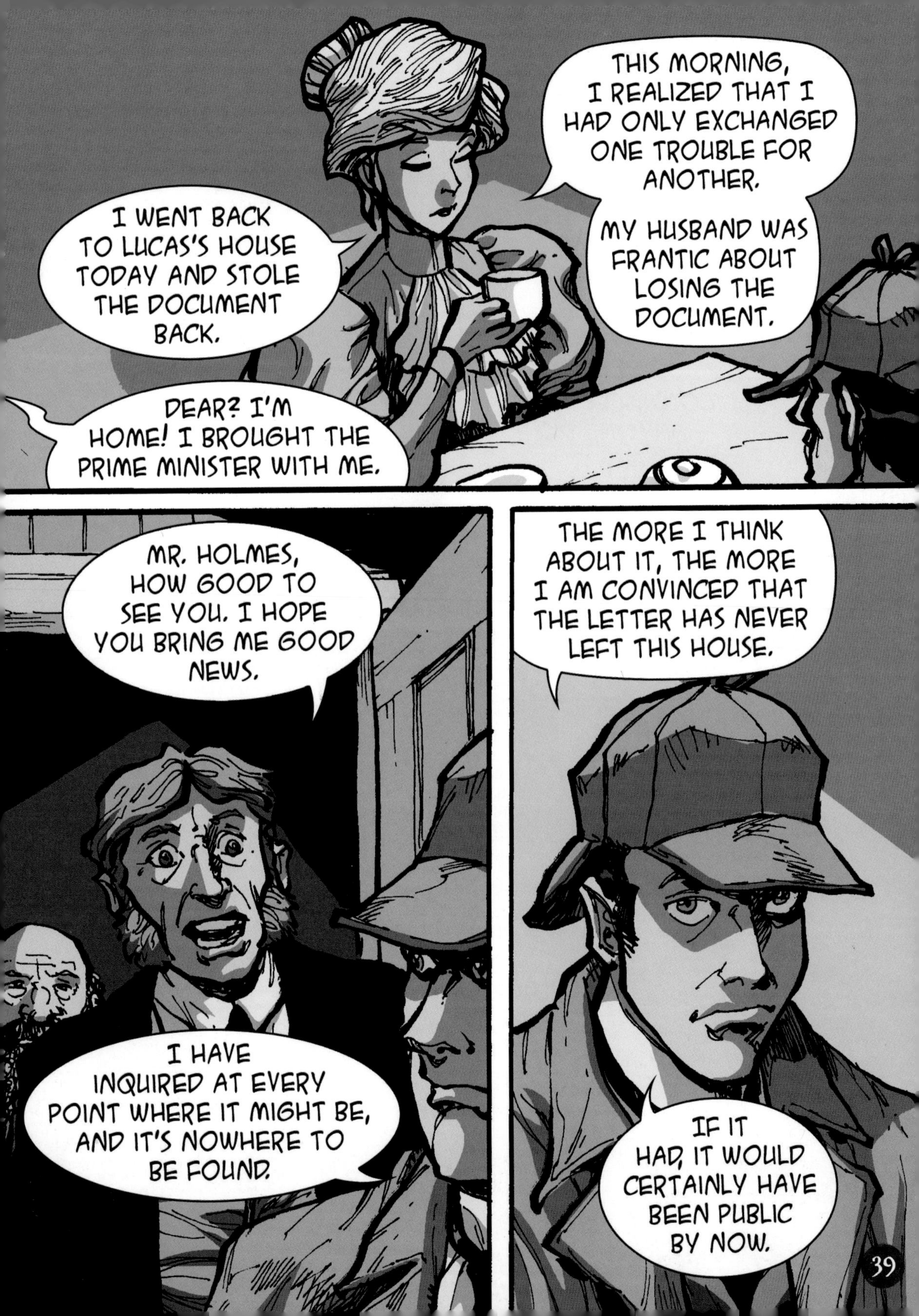

I WENT BACK TO LUCAS'S HOUSE TODAY AND STOLE THE DOCUMENT BACK.
THIS MORNING, I REALIZED THAT I HAD ONLY EXCHANGED ONE TROUBLE FOR ANOTHER.
MY HUSBAND WAS FRANTIC ABOUT LOSING THE DOCUMENT.
DEAR? I'M HOME! I BROUGHT THE PRIME MINISTER WITH ME.
MR. HOLMES, HOW GOOD TO SEE YOU. I HOPE YOU BRING ME GOOD NEWS.
I HAVE INQUIRED AT EVERY POINT WHERE IT MIGHT BE, AND IT'S NOWHERE TO BE FOUND.
THE MORE I THINK ABOUT IT, THE MORE I AM CONVINCED THAT THE LETTER HAS NEVER LEFT THIS HOUSE.
IF IT HAD, IT WOULD CERTAINLY HAVE BEEN PUBLIC BY NOW.

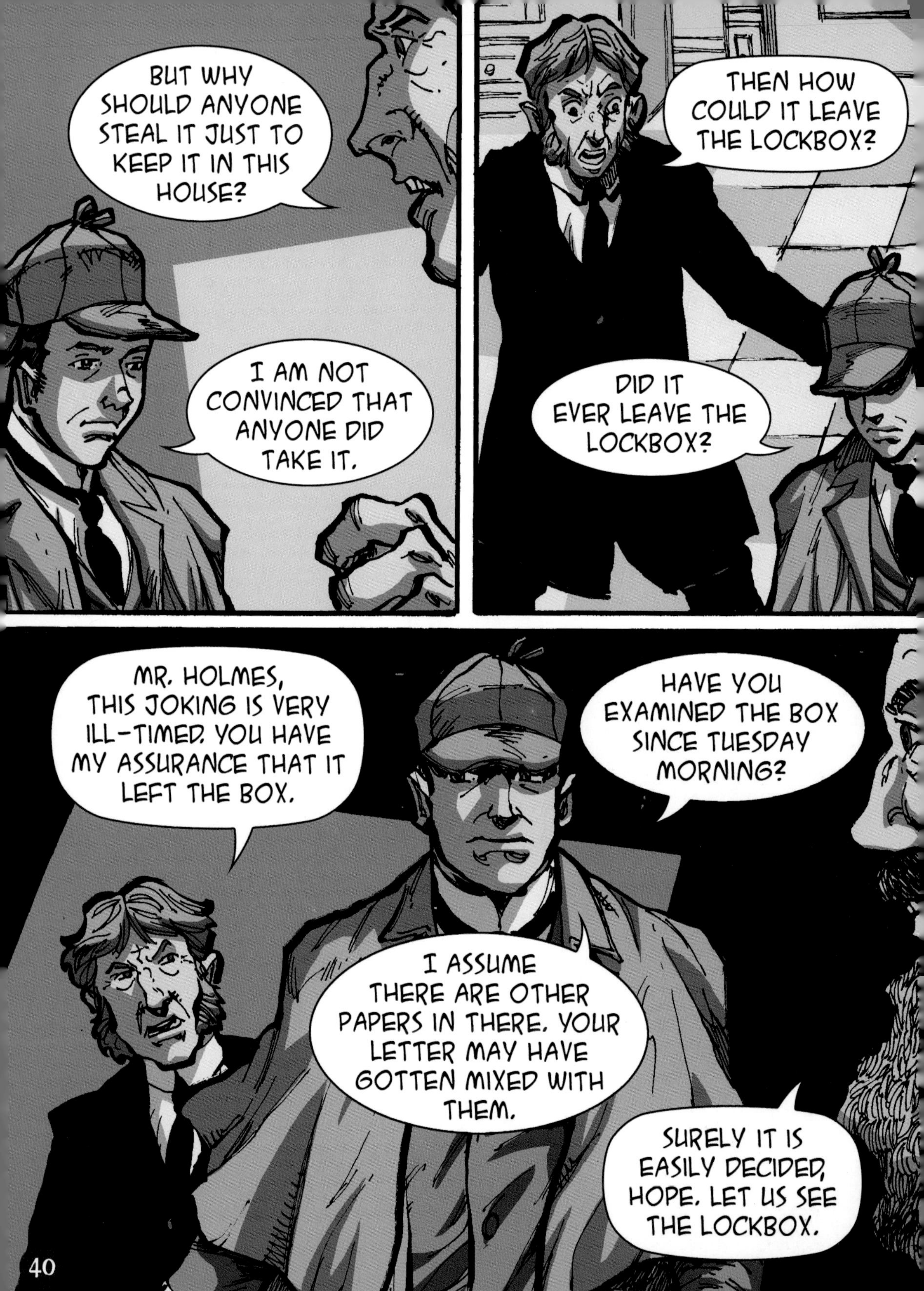
BUT WHY SHOULD ANYONE STEAL IT JUST TO KEEP IT IN THIS HOUSE?
I AM NOT CONVINCED THAT ANYONE DID TAKE IT.
THEN HOW COULD IT LEAVE THE LOCKBOX?
DID IT EVER LEAVE THE LOCKBOX?
MR. HOLMES, THIS JOKING IS VERY ILL-TIMED. YOU HAVE MY ASSURANCE THAT IT LEFT THE BOX.
HAVE YOU EXAMINED THE BOX SINCE TUESDAY MORNING?
I ASSUME THERE ARE OTHER PAPERS IN THERE. YOUR LETTER MAY HAVE GOTTEN MIXED WITH THEM.
SURELY IT IS EASILY DECIDED, HOPE. LET US SEE THE LOCKBOX.

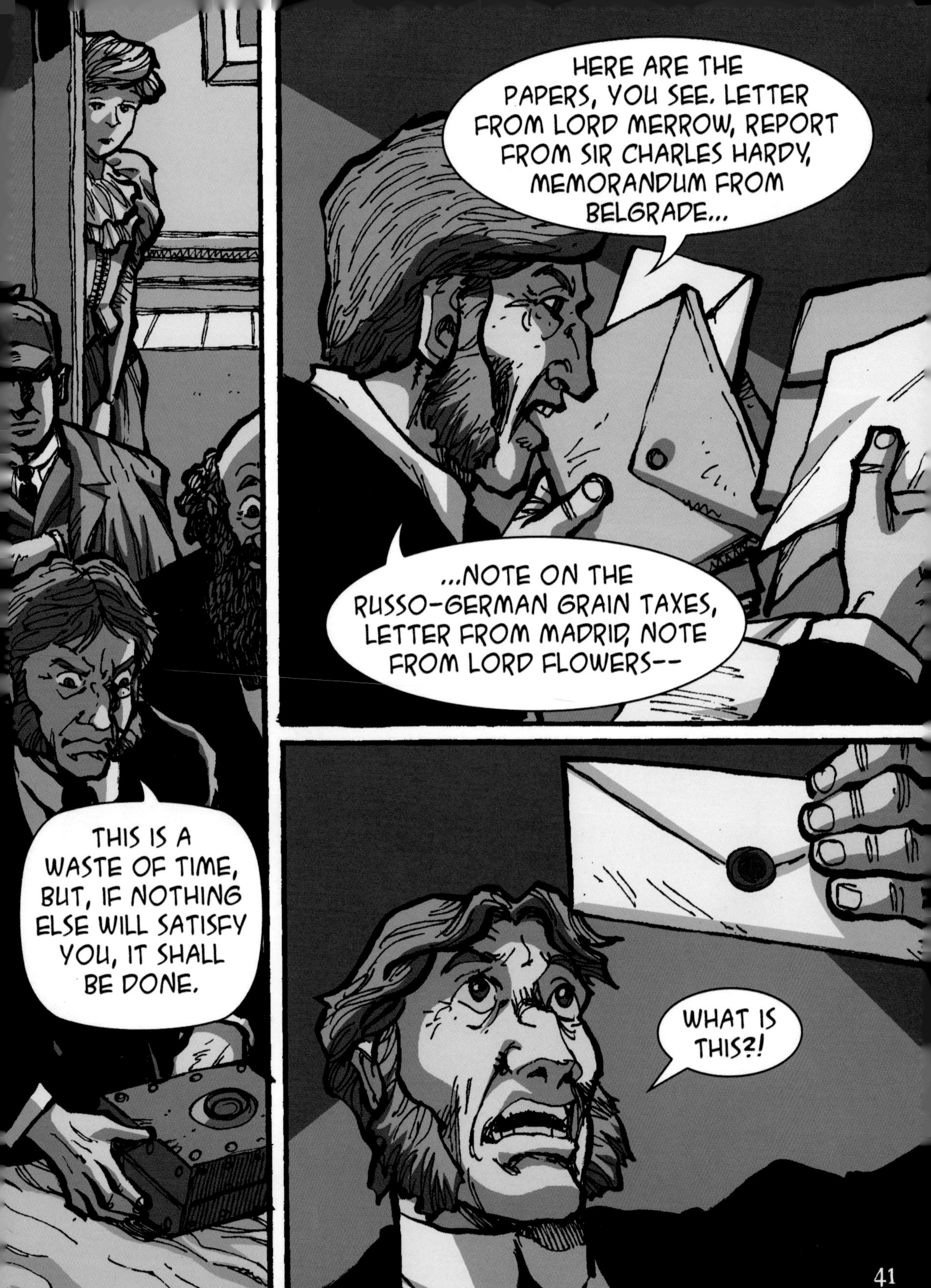
HERE ARE THE PAPERS, YOU SEE. LETTER FROM LORD MERROW, REPORT FROM SIR CHARLES HARDY, MEMORANDUM FROM BELGRADE...
...NOTE ON THE RUSSO-GERMAN GRAIN TAXES, LETTER FROM MADRID, NOTE FROM LORD FLOWERS--
THIS IS A WASTE OF TIME, BUT, IF NOTHING ELSE WILL SATISFY YOU, IT SHALL BE DONE.
WHAT IS THIS?!

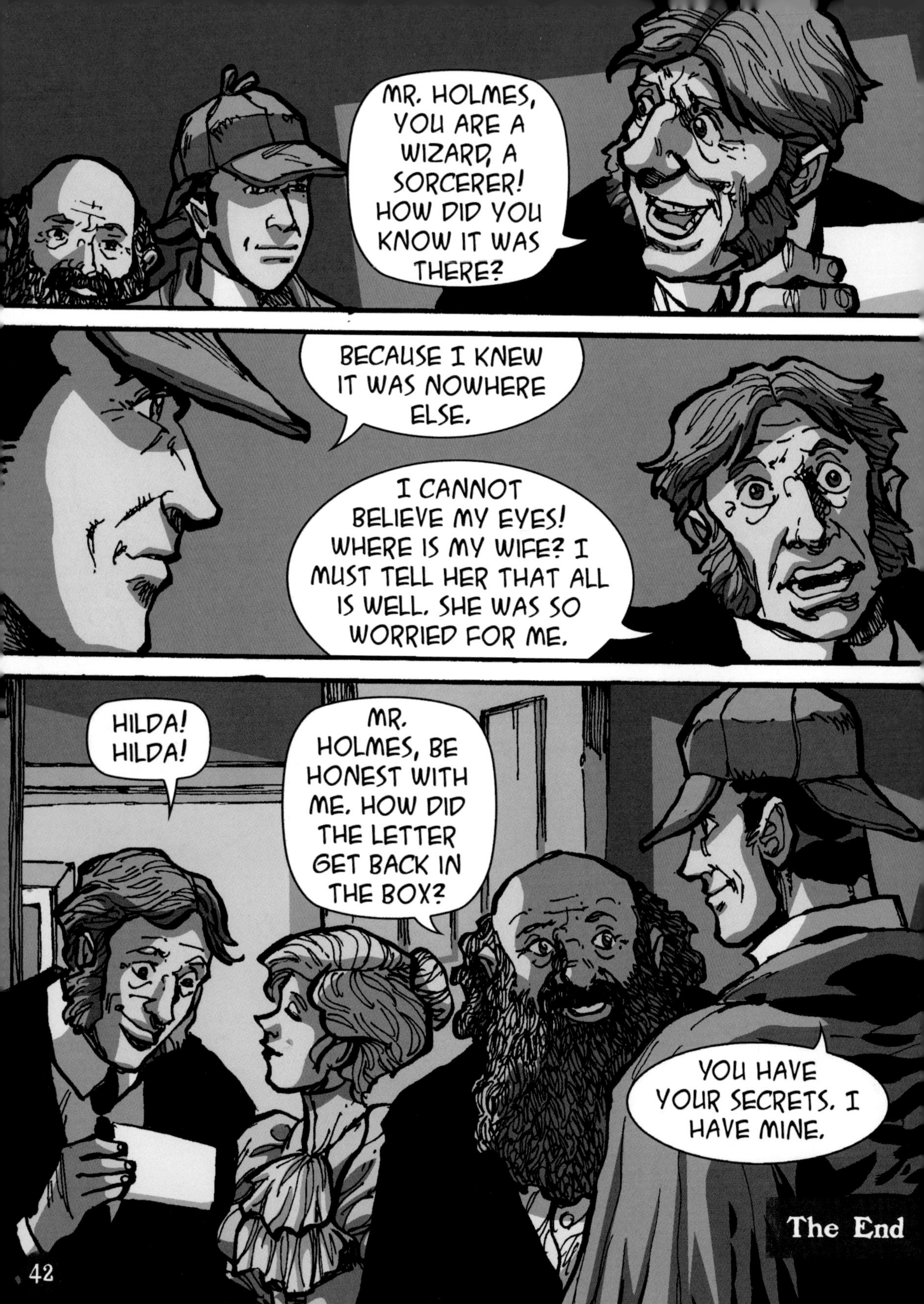
MR. HOLMES, YOU ARE A WIZARD, A SORCERER! HOW DID YOU KNOW IT WAS THERE?
BECAUSE I KNEW IT WAS NOWHERE ELSE.
I CANNOT BELIEVE MY EYES! WHERE IS MY WIFE? I MUST TELL HER THAT ALL IS WELL. SHE WAS SO WORRIED FOR ME.
HILDA! HILDA!
MR. HOLMES, BE HONEST WITH ME. HOW DID THE LETTER GET BACK IN THE BOX?
YOU HAVE YOUR SECRETS. I HAVE MINE.
The End

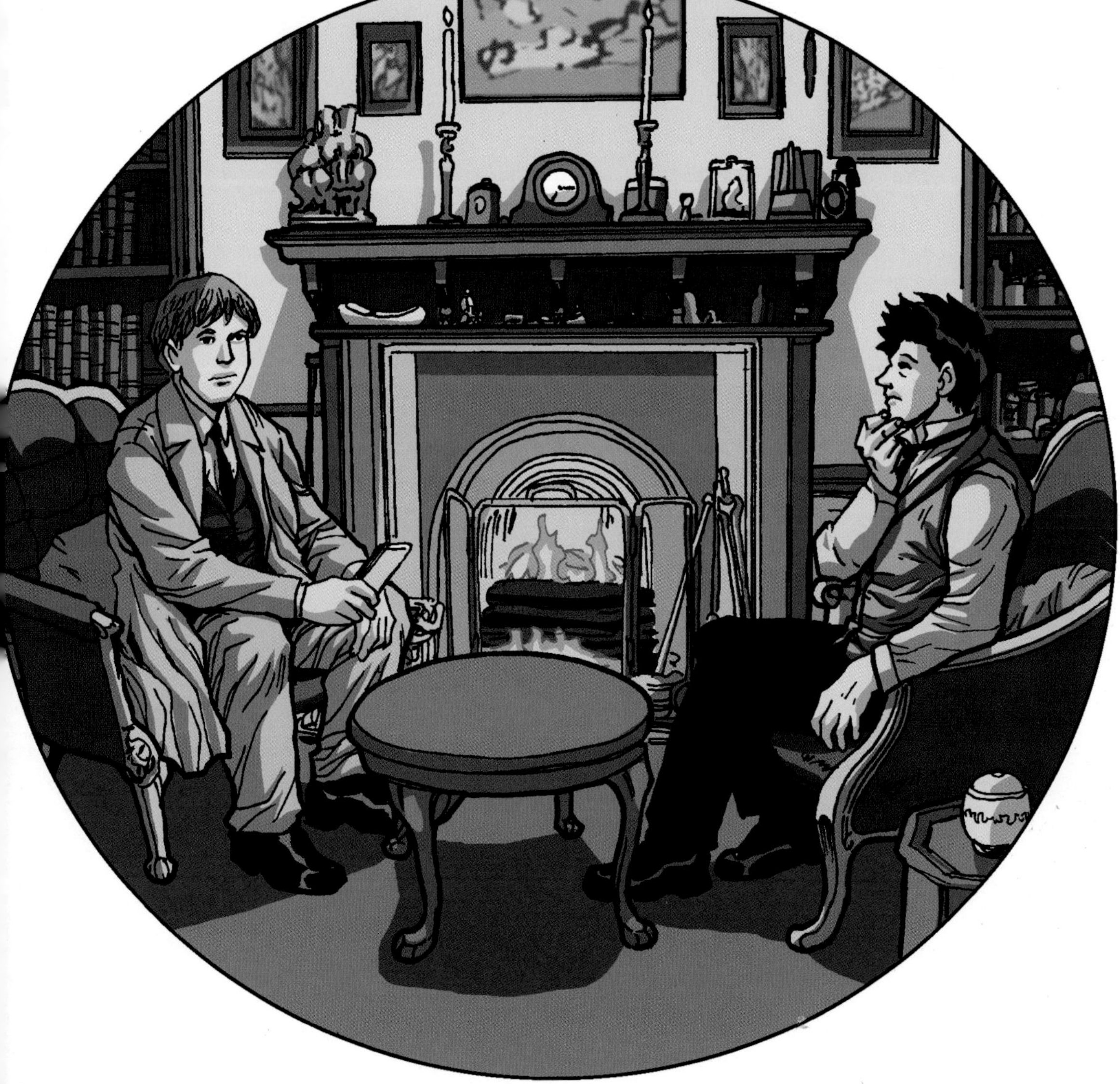

How to Draw
Dr. John Watson

by Ben Dunn

Step 1: Use a pencil to draw a simple framework. You can start with a stick figure! Then add circles, ovals, and cylinders to get the basic form. Getting the simple shapes in place is the beginning to solving any great case.

Step 2: Time to add to Watson's look. Use the shapes you started with to fill in his clothes. Use guidelines to add circles for the eyes. And don't forget to make sure the hat covers the head, not floats on top of it.

Step 3: Now you can go in with a pen and start inking Watson. Fill in all the details and fix any mistakes. Let the ink dry to avoid smudges, then erase any pencil marks. Watson is ready for some color, so grab your markers and get started!

Glossary

confidence - the state of being sure of oneself.

consequence - the result, effect, or outcome of something.

delusion - something that is falsely believed to be true.

desperate - having a great need.

dire - likely to cause fear or harm; looking to be bad; grim.

embarrassed - feeling ashamed or uncomfortable.

inquiries - questions.

naught - nothing.

scandal - an action that shocks people and disgraces those connected with it.

telegram - a coded message sent by electricity over wires.

Web Sites

To learn more about Sir Arthur Conan Doyle, visit ABDO Group online at **www.abdopublishing.com.** Web sites about Doyle are featured on our Book Links page. These links are routinely monitored and updated to provide the most current information available.

Arthur Conan Doyle was born on May 22, 1859, in Edinburgh, Scotland. He was the second of Charles Altamont and Mary Foley Doyle's ten children. In 1868, Doyle began his schooling in England. Eight years later, he returned to Scotland.

Upon his return, Doyle entered the University of Edinburgh's medical school, where he became a doctor in 1885. That year, he married Louisa Hawkins. Together they had two children.

While a medical student, Doyle was impressed when his professor observed the tiniest details of a patient's condition. Doyle later wrote stories where his most famous character, Sherlock Holmes, used this same technique to solve mysteries. Holmes first appeared in *A Study in Scarlet* in 1887 and was immediately popular.

Between 1887 and 1927, Doyle wrote 66 stories and 3 novels about Holmes. He also wrote other fiction and nonfiction novels throughout his life. In 1902, Doyle was knighted for his work in a field hospital in the South African War. Four years later, Louisa died. Doyle married Jean Leckie in 1907, and they had three children together.

Sir Arthur Conan Doyle died on July 7, 1930, in Sussex, England. Today, Doyle's famous character, Sherlock Holmes, is honored with societies around the world that pay tribute to the detective.

Additional Works

A Study in Scarlet (1887)

The Mystery of Cloomber (1889)

The Firm of Girdlestone (1890)

The White Company (1891)

The Adventures of Sherlock Holmes (1891-92)

The Memoirs of Sherlock Holmes (1892-93)

Round the Red Lamp (1894)

The Stark Munro Letters (1895)

The Great Boer War (1900)

The Hound of the Baskervilles (1901-02)

The Return of Sherlock Holmes (1903-04)

Through the Magic Door (1907)

The Crime of the Congo (1909)

The Coming of the Fairies (1922)

Memories and Adventures (1924)

The Case-Book of Sherlock Holmes (1921-1927)

About the Adapters

Author

Vincent Goodwin earned his BA in Drama and Communications from Trinity University in San Antonio. He is the writer of three plays as well as the cowriter of the comic book *Pirates vs. Ninjas II.* Goodwin is also an accomplished journalist, having won several awards for his work as a columnist and reporter.

Illustrator

Ben Dunn founded Antarctic Press, one of the largest comic companies in the United States. His works appear in Marvel and Image comics. He is best known for his series *Ninja High School* and *Warrior Nun Areala.*